LaJOYCE MARTIN

MISTRESS OF Magnolia manor

Mistress of Magnolia Manor

by LaJoyce Martin

© 2002, Word Aflame Press
Hazelwood, MO 63042-2299

ISBN 1-56722-620-5

Cover Design by Paul Povolni

All Scripture quotations in this book are from the King James Version of the Bible unless otherwise identified.

Printed in United States of America

Printed by

WORD AFLAME®PRESS
8855 DUNN ROAD
HAZELWOOD, MO 63042-2299

Contents

Book One

CHAPTER ONE

The First-born

"Have you been crying again, Helen?" The edge of Emrick's voice tattled that his sympathy was wearing thin.

Helen's hands flew to her face. She had tried to take the puffiness from her swollen eyelids with cold spoons. She'd dabbed her red nose with flour. But she hadn't fooled Emrick.

Crying was a daily ritual, an inveterate addiction. And Emrick was tired of it. She couldn't blame him, but neither could she cap the flow of tears from the inner geyser. If she dammed them, her heart might rupture.

Helen Teff's thirteen-year spate of tears was not for physical pain. Her husband didn't abuse her, nor had she a terminal disease or a lack of rudimentary comforts. Her sorrow—and it was constant—was a heartache, the pang of an unfulfilled yearning. She identified with Hannah in the Bible. With Sarah. With Rachel. She wanted children.

"Am I not enough for you?" her husband, Emrick, had

asked even as Elkanah had questioned centuries before. Helen allowed that Emrick was the best spouse any woman could wish. Certainly he had his faults, but they were inconsequential. He tried hard enough to make her happy. How could a woman tell her husband that, no, he wasn't enough to plug the abyss of loneliness in her spirit? Could a man understand the maternal craving for a child of one's own? Indeed, he could not.

Helen, a fetching lass of eighteen when she met Emrick, was an only child and orphaned at that. "When I am married, I shall have *scads* of youngsters," she enthused. "I shall spend hours cooking for them and sewing for them, and I shall take time to play with them!"

They were wed, and the years marched by—one, two, three, four, five—and alarm encroached. There were no babies. Helen cried and prayed and hoped. And cried more. Her tears, she reckoned, would fill a horse trough.

She and Emrick graduated from a neat, one-room log cabin near the borough of Sommerville to a spreading ranch house. Emrick bought land. And more land. He named his place Paradise Ranch. Everything he set his hands to prospered: crops, raising livestock, the gristmill. He was busy and content. Helen felt empty and discontent.

Couldn't they go down to the orphan train? Helen eventually suggested. They would pick a youngster or two and give them a home, a chance.

No! Absolutely not! Emrick balked. They might get a bad-blooded one. He had heard that the street children on the trains were unappreciative, rebellious, insubordinate, and that they often ran away after you'd invested time and money in them. If God wanted them to have a child, He

10

would give them one. Otherwise, they would do without. Period.

Afterward, when he stretched, long and shoeless, in an easy chair and said, "Helen, we have it mighty cozy here, haven't we? We're blessed!" she would want to retort: "No, we are cursed, cursed with childlessness!"

Then after thirteen years of tears, it happened. At age thirty-one, Helen Teff bore a puny and sickly son. Her joy knew no bounds. Now it was time for thirteen years of laughter. Egypt had their good years first, followed by an equal season of famine. Well, Helen Teff was doing things backward. Her years of starving for a child were passed. It was time for feasting.

To wake to the hymn of hens and the tabering of turtledoves and to lay a sleep-weakened hand on the rounded blanket in the basket beside her bed gave Helen such happiness she wanted to shout.

It didn't matter that her baby cried around the clock or spit up his milk. He was hers, possessing her body and soul. He was the world's most brilliant baby, destined for great achievements.

She named him Atlas.

CHAPTER TWO

A Restless Lad

Atlas left behind the colic but retained a colicky disposition. He was a morose lad, keeping the hatches of his thoughts battened down tightly. He did not like the ranch. He saw cities with high-rise buildings biting the sky and banners of smoke floating above the metropolis. Then he gazed about the ranch, where morning wore to night in a never-ending march of hard chore upon hard chore, and he groaned between his set teeth. An expression of settled abstraction came into his face, and he was often silent, brooding.

Little things irritated the boy. Like the sight of his father's overalls worn the day before lying over the back of the rocker, chaff spilling from the cuffs. They looked like weary clothes, weary with a farmer's tiredness. Who wanted to be saddled with broken-down wagons, parching droughts, biting frosts, heartbreaking toil, and the endless struggle to survive? There had to be a better life. . . .

If Helen noticed, she must have considered the melancholic moods of Atlas normal. She went about her accustomed tasks with none other thought than the duties of the moment. God had given her the son for which she had prayed, and any complaint would be a form of blasphemy. Thus she wielded her broom and made her corn pone while she sang, "My blessings are more than I can count." Meanwhile, Emrick worked harder, improved his land, and added to his herds.

Time flew by, and Atlas plunged headlong into adolescence, hale and hearty—and exceedingly spoiled. The white fire of rebellion leaped mutinously in his heart. A leaven was working.

He had no plans of serving his life sentence in this prison. When his father, upon whom the infirmities of age were already creeping, was gone, he would sell the place and answer the loud clarion that called to him from beyond the horizons. The fences could not hold him. "You can't keep a river from the ocean," he counseled himself. "That's the difference between a river and a pond. Ponds stagnate. Rivers run. I shall not stay around to stagnate."

Only once did Atlas bare the abscess in his mind to his father. That was when the unceasing ferment became a torment. "When I grow up, I want more than a herd of mindless cows and a few thousand rocks to stump my toes upon when I try to plow," he growled. "I'm tired of drudgery! I want *big* rewards. If I were you, Papa, I would sell this place and—"

"I don't need any cub of a boy telling me what to do!" Emrick thundered. "I am nigh to fifty years old, and I have provided well for my family all this while. I had brains aplenty to run this ranch before you were born. I lack for

14

nothing, your mother lacks for nothing, and you lack for nothing. Now go to bed—and be quick about it!"

The lad made no move to obey. Emrick strode toward him threateningly, and Helen covered her face with her hands. "No, Emrick!" she begged. "Do not strike him!"

"Did you hear what I said, Atlas?" Emrick demanded. "Are you going yourself, or shall I take you upstairs?"

Slowly Atlas rose to his feet. "I'll go," he said evenly, "but I've a few more things to say when your temper is past."

"We will never discuss the matter again!" Emrick flared, his chest rising and falling with his anger. "Go to bed!"

Atlas disappeared up the stairway, leaving the room suddenly quiet, so quiet that the buzz of a fly, unnoticed before, now dominated it. Then from Helen's chair came a sound that hinted at secret weeping.

At last she spoke from her heart. "Atlas is an unquenchable flame, Emrick," she said, one notch above a whisper. "Don't force him to smolder until he bursts into blaze."

"Everything has been quiet and peaceable until now," shot Emrick, "and I don't expect it to change because of an ungrateful child. Atlas is pampered. I'm afraid it is all our fault." His tired face bore the effects of a vexed spirit.

Helen came and knelt at his knee. "Please, Emrick. He is our only son. He is our—future. It is Atlas who will wear the harness in the years ahead. It is Atlas who will care for us in our old age."

Emrick took her hand and held it. When she was young, she turned his head. As he aged, she turned his heart. "Is this place not good enough for you, dear?" The words came out a little brokenly, catching on snags of concern.

"It is fine," she whispered.

"Do you want to sell it and move to the city with rattling milk wagons, bawdy saloons, and noisy neighbors?"

"No, no, Emrick! But the boy is young and . . . and turned differently than you and I."

Emrick's hands shook. "I can't keep up the ranch without help, Helen. I am playing out. Some days I feel as though I'm sitting at the edge of time with my feet dangling into eternity."

"Don't say that, Emrick. You're still strong and healthy—and very handsome." She patted his knee. "Just don't push so hard. You're wearing yourself out. Small wonder the boy doesn't want to follow in your footsteps. We can do on less."

"What—what if Atlas should grow up and decide to leave us?"

"He'll stay, Emrick. He won't desert us. . . ."

Sadness smoldered in the man's faded eyes. "What's good enough for the old blood doesn't always satisfy the new, Helen. We're looking back, and life runs forward. If the boy's heart isn't in it—"

Helen's only answer was a sigh, and Emrick continued. "The ranch is debt free, and we've laid enough by to live in comfort for several years. I just can't think of selling our home."

"Don't fret so, dear. By morning, Atlas will have changed his mind," the mother said. "Often a boy goes to sleep and awakens with quite a changed notion. It is a trait of his age; I've talked to other mothers who have encountered the same problem. You were much too hard on him. How can a fourteen-year-old know his own mind? All youngsters go through stages, and this is but a stage, a boy's restlessness. Some days he is a boy-man and other days he is a man-boy. We've not been o'er the path of rearing a half-boy, half-man. We must have patience. Another few years, and he will realize how blessed he is."

"You are right, of course, Helen," Emrick conceded. "But you must realize that the boy hit a sore spot when he spoke of selling Paradise Ranch. We planted those morning glory vines there in the yard when first we wed, and I want to stay here and enjoy them until we die."

"We will, Emrick," she said, snuggling closer to him. "We will."

But upstairs, Atlas thrashed between the freshly laundered sheets while his waking dreams flung great cities before his eyes, beckoning him, calling to him. His spirit was the spirit of a hatching eaglet impatiently pecking at the shell which too slowly opens to freedom.

CHAPTER THREE

The Surprise

Atlas said nothing more about the roiling within his heart. He worked steadily and faithfully, turning out the work of two men. Time was his advocate. *I'm the sole heir to the Teff fortune*, he reminded himself daily, if not hourly, *and my parents are over the hill.*

Then the unexpected happened. When he was nearing sixteen, Helen was forty-six, and Emrick fifty-two, Helen bore a set of twins. The boy, a listless and tiny form, lived only a few hours, swallowed without a name by the earth. But the girl, lusty and strong, thrived joyfully, filling the house with her presence. A gurgling, happy infant, she was her father's delight, absorbing his attention and bringing happiness such as had never descended on Paradise Ranch. Emrick named her Emma Joy, the "Emma" in his own honor and the "Joy" for his rapture.

However, the late-life birth took a dastardly toll on Helen's deteriorating health, and she took to her grave before Emma was weaned. Emrick was inconsolable.

How would he manage without his Helen?

When the deep, shocking spasm of grief was gone and he got his head about him again, he hired a nurse until Emma's need for milk was outgrown, then cared for the child himself, taking her everywhere he went: to the fields, to town, to church. "He don't trust nobody else with the biddy," retorted a neighbor. "Ain't never seen a pa so maudlin over a saplin'."

The lack of a mother seemed to distress Emma not at all. She blossomed under her father's watchful eye. "Papa" was the only vocabulary word she needed.

From babyhood, Emma was uncommonly pretty. Her golden hair glowed between the extremes of amber and tawny copper; her expressive eyes were a velvety violet and deeply vivid. Everyone who saw her raved over her astounding beauty. A natural-born charmer she was.

But Atlas resented Emma from the onset. Now he would have to share the inheritance, and the idea galled him. He would be the drone and do all the work. She'd be the queen bee, doing nothing while collecting half the honey. He paid his sister scant notice though, heaven knows, she tried hard to include him in her goodwill and cheer.

More and more of the raw chores of the farm fell to Atlas as more and more of his father's time became usurped by the girl. When his studies were done, Atlas fell into bed exhausted in body and mind only to be awakened at dawn to retread the dread duties: only that and nothing more. With determined effort, he finished his education at the top of his class.

So engrossed was Emrick in Emma's childish antics that Atlas's growing dudgeon went unnoticed. It was

20

inconceivable that anyone could not adore his small goddess. He neglected his work to fill her every whim.

Atlas shouldered the load, working long and hard. His interest was not, however, ranching; it was in keeping the place primed for sale. Age was ravishing his father. Atlas would soon be at the head of the line.

Circumstances improved when Emma started day school. After Emrick fed the child her breakfast of "mixed-up-stirred" (butter and sugar creamed and spread on two halves of a biscuit) or "bo-hole-y" (a biscuit with a hole punched in the side and molasses poured in), he delivered her to the schoolhouse door—and was waiting for her when the dismissal bell rang. The hours between gave him some time for planting, plowing, and reaping. But his mind was nonetheless distracted.

Emma suffered the usual childhood ailments, sending Emrick into fits of worry. Atlas thought the doctor came too often and charged too much, but he judiciously held his tongue. He would not have grieved if the child had expired with the mumps or chicken pox or whooping cough. But she proved stronger than the diseases that befell her, wending her way through them all unscathed.

For one blessing Atlas could be thankful. Emma sponged up all Emrick's affections, and he had none left for the hopeful spinsters and widows who swarmed him like buzzards. A second wife could complicate matters for Atlas. The birth of Emma had botched his plans badly enough. Another hand in the dishpan could be fatal to his hopes.

Atlas had no social life. This was by choice. Considered a "good catch" by the local girls, he knew himself pursued, but he sidestepped the conspirators. *There will be time enough for courting when I reach New York or St. Louis or Philadelphia—or wherever I choose to settle,* he told himself. *I'll find high-class ladies there. Moneyed gals. Love is secondary. Wealth is the essence of life.*

The first niggle of a concrete plan was growing on Atlas's mind like a slow-spreading fungus. He would need to find some way to cut his sister from the inheritance. But how?

CHAPTER FOUR

Papa's Plan

Atlas was an opportunist. He recognized and seized opportunities when they came. And the chance he sought came presently.

Emrick not only did less and less work, but he also took to his bed more and more frequently. He was not well. Helen's death had broken the mainspring of his life, and only Emma kept him "ticking."

In his room, Atlas lay awake sorting facts and laying them in a row much like he had culled seeds from his apple and counted them as a child. He did not know when consciousness became unconsciousness nor what startled him to wakefulness.

There was a sound in the night, and the young man found himself sitting straight and tense, his eyes boring the dark, his ears straining to hear, his whole body taut as he listened. The sound came again.

Presently, Atlas rose and reached for the candle stand, moving with sure and soundless feet to his father's room across the hallway. The clock struck five. The veil of night soon would be lifting from the face of the world.

"Atlas!" Emrick called his son to his bedside.

"Yes, Papa?"

Emrick turned toward his son slowly and resolutely. With his candle held low, Atlas recognized the strange gray death in his father's eyes.

"What's on your mind, Papa?" he asked with forced patience. In the glow of the flame, his eyes took in the portrait on the bureau, a tintype of his mother, her lovely face vivid even in the blur of the long-ago photography. He bore her likeness.

Beside the bed sat Emrick's worn boots. He had money to buy dozens of pairs of new ones, but the old man was tightfisted, thrifty.

Emrick's Bible lay open on a chair with a scripture underlined. "Read it," Emrick pointed to the open Book.

Atlas read: "For they have sown the wind, and they shall reap the whirlwind: it hath no stalk: the bud shall yield no meal: if so be it yield, the strangers shall swallow it up."

"I don't know why God directed me to that scripture, Atlas. Perhaps it is for you."

Thoughts clashed within Atlas, dark and bitter meditations. He felt an unreasonable defiance rising in him. He would brook no preaching from the old man. "If this is why you called me—"

"It is about the ranch that I want to speak, Atlas."

"Yes?" he responded coldly.

"My days are numbered, son. Something is eating at my innards, and I am losing flesh. Blood is leaving my body daily. You are strong and healthy."

"I know everything there is to know about ranching, Papa. I can raise cattle. I can run the mill. I can bundle hay. I can make money. You are not to worry."

"I know that you can. You have proven that to me, and I'm glad."

"I know the markets. Prices are on the rise." Pride was settling like cold grease in Atlas, intrinsic in the moment.

"I know, I know, Atlas." Emrick's hand slashed the dark with an impatient gesture. "It isn't for you that I trouble myself. Young men such as yourself are strong and able, invincible. It is with the gentler gender that we must concern ourselves. It is Emma's future that plagues my mind."

"Leave everything to me."

"I have a plan, Atlas. You can make your own way in life. I started at your age with forty acres and a hand tiller. From there to where I am now hasn't been so very long when you stop to count the years. It gives one a sense of personal accomplishment to go from small to great, from poor to plenty. There is no feeling like it. I want you to experience it as I did. The back forty has a little cabin and good water.

"Emma is a girl. Girls must be cared for, protected. We menfolk can rough it. Ladyfolk can't. I will leave you the forty acres of land, a plow, and enough money to put in your first crop."

"Papa, I—"

"Yes, I recall that you wanted another life. Well, you are free to sell your forty acres and work in a factory for ten cents an hour. It is your choice.

"But the rest of the property must go to little Emma, who is neither old enough nor strong enough to meet her tomorrow. There are resources aplenty to keep her for many years. Of course, you may work the land for her until she is of age—and divide the profit. That would only be fair.

"What I want you to do is get me a lawyer out here so that I can draw up legal papers to that effect."

"Yes, Papa. I'll get you a lawyer." Atlas struggled to hide the anger that hectored his nerves.

"Soon, Atlas."

"Yes, Papa."

Hate, like a belch of filth, arose in Atlas. His heels came down hard on the wooden floor as he left the room.

CHAPTER FIVE

Cecile's Decision

Cecile Dunmore, occupying a hardwood bench in the Sommerville coach house, awaited the westbound stage while still wondering if she had done the right thing. It was a foolish decision, really. Or was it? She had traveled from Alabama to Arkansas, and there were two states to cross yet.

She unfolded the much-handled letter from her husband and read it once again.

Dear Cecile:

I am missing you, my darling. I long to have you with me, but I would not ask you to leave the comforts of the plantation to join me. This wilderness is no place for a lady.

How long I will be away I do not know, but I must stay until I find peace within myself, until I can cease blaming God for our loss. Only then can I be the support that you need—and deserve. Forgive me for being less of a man than I should be.

This part of the country is different but lovely in its solitude. The stars, in the vastness of the night sky, are close overhead . . . and alive. The air is dry and light, always offering a fresh breeze. I feel nearer to God here, and I talk with Him often. I am healing. Please be patient with me.

Give my regards to Cecil and Sarah, the best in-laws in the world. Had I not felt that your father was capable of running the plantation with the greatest of efficiency, I would not have left. I am assured that all is going well in my absence.

Avail yourself of anything you need, my dear Cecile. You are in my heart every moment, and I yearn for the day we are together again.

Devotedly,
Blake

Cecile folded the letter slowly and returned it to her handbag, stroking the handle of her silk parasol without conscious thought. Blake had no idea she was on her way. A sudden call on her heart urged her to the hasty arrangements to join him. Her mother, Sarah, had sputtered, fretting for her safety in that "waste howling wilderness" of the New Mexico territory.

"It is a very dangerous land!" she had warned. "There are coyotes and hyenas and Gila monsters and rattlers out there. Please, Cecile!"

But Cecile was not to be deterred. So lonely was she for her husband that life had become meaningless without him. *Better to die trying to reach my Blake than to live in this misery,* she reasoned.

It wasn't for gold that Blake Dunmore had left

Magnolia Manor, or even for adventure. Blake was running from his grief, from memories, trying to outdistance the shattering sorrow that had dropped upon him. His only child, Anna, had developed a fever and died, leaving Blake's heart battered and bleeding. Everywhere he looked about the plantation, he "saw" her: in the hassock, at the table, running down the path, riding her pony.

Cecile's grief was no less intense than his, but she was better able to cope with it. What must be borne in life must be borne, she calculated, and to go to pieces would only heap upon Blake a greater burden. The man had suffered many more losses in life than herself, and emotion stacked on emotion was a dangerous thing.

So Blake had gone, as Cecile supposed "for a few days." But the days had turned to weeks, and the weeks to months. She could no longer bear his absence. She would find him and bring him home to Magnolia Manor again.

Blake's father, Woodward Dunmore, had purchased the eighteen-hundred-acre plantation in Alabama's deep south in 1865 for two thousand dollars in gold. Blake, his only son, fell heir to it. Cecile admired Magnolia Manor so much that Blake said she would have married him just to live there.

Set amongst massive trees and with a sweeping lawn, the impressive mansion had dignity and character. Great chimneys, handmade brick walls, and magnificent windows with deep reveals and handsome woodwork lent themselves to its charm. In the spring, purple wisteria draped its clusters over the sills, filling the atmosphere with a warm, honeyed fragrance.

Anna was buried beneath a scuppernong arbor, a shrub-bordered walk leading to the grave site. The path was hard packed by the many daily trips of Cecile's feet. Before he left, Blake placed a stone bench in the cove so that she might sit in solitude near her child's tomb. The doctor said there would be no more children.

Cecile had been hurt when Blake went away, bruised in her spirit that he left her to endure her grief alone. But gradually she came to understand that his brutal emotions had driven him to flee, that the loss of his beloved Anna was more than he could handle. Her pain turned to sympathy and her sympathy to compassion.

The plantation had several permanent employees, and their duties were "fossilized" as Blake put it. There were a cook, a housekeeper, a gardener, and a bevy of field hands. Most of them were there before Cecile. She was just a figurehead, so to speak. Therefore, as Mistress of the house, she had no compunctions about leaving. Magnolia Manor would run smoothly while she was gone just as it did before she came.

After rereading Blake's latest letter, Cecile felt better. At least half of her journey was behind her, and all in all, it hadn't been a bad trip. Granted, some of the stopovers were less than commodious, many gave but beggarly lodging, but when one had a goal, one could brave most anything. And she hadn't been coddled with a silver-spoon upbringing.

Sommerville was one of the nicer inns. She glanced at the big clock with its slow swinging pendulum. Three hours until the next coach . . .

A chill of excitement ran down her spine. In a few days, she would be with Blake!

CHAPTER SIX

The Questioning

*W*hy, *God? Why?*

Here he was questioning again!

Blake Dunmore stood in the door of his soddie, looking east. All of the yesterdays—the happy ones and the sad ones—paraded across his mind, bringing yet more soul-searching. The raking of his soul had left the bare rocks of bitterness exposed.

He had known no deprivation for the sum of his thirty-six years, but the paucity of the wilderness bothered him little. A kettle, a coffeepot, and a cast-iron skillet sufficed. His mirror, which revealed the ravages of sorrow, was a bucket of clear water. What need had he for life's comforts now that his child was sleeping in the cold earth?

Back and back Blake's thoughts traveled, back to the cozy cottage of his birth, his home until his father acquired Magnolia Manor. The cottage was one and one-half stories with dormer windows and a gabled portico. In the front yard grew a crab apple tree as tall as the house itself. In the spring, the tree might have been a giant's bouquet of pink blossoms. His mother's only objection to leaving "the wee house" for "the big house" was parting with her tree. He could see his mother now in her blue tea gown and his father hurrying home from the fields to play catch with him before dusk. He was seven years old when they moved. In a dozen years, both of his parents had died, hurling the responsibility of the plantation on his young shoulders.

He had met Cecile quite by accident. Her home in Morgan County had been burned by federal troops, and her family wandered about as itinerant laborers, never able to recover financially.

Cecile and her mother were sitting beside the road with the disabled wagon that held all their earthly possessions while Cecil Eden, Cecile's father, went into town to repair the broken wheel. Blake stopped to offer assistance. When he saw Cecile, it was love at first sight.

He hired Mr. Eden on the spot, readying one of the servant's quarters for the family's lodging. His motive was to keep Cecile in sight. He married her the following year and moved her into Magnolia Manor, inviting her parents into the manor, too. They insisted they would be more content in their small dwelling so as not to be underfoot.

Sarah, Cecile's mother, loved flowers. She cultivated an elaborate rose garden and prided herself in being able to call her specimens by name: Malmaison. Lamark. General Jacqueminot. Safrano. Red Odeheat. Giant of Battles. Yellow Harrison. Solfetaire. Pearl of the Garden. Gloire Dijon. Pink Daily. Madam Joseph Schwartz.

Cecil Eden, on the other hand, favored vegetables. Something grew year-round. There were shallots and parsley. Mint for tea and tarts. Beets, peas, and butter beans proliferated under his coaxing. Asparagus and strawberry beds prospered, along with raspberries, figs, plums, apricots, and horse apples.

Blake adopted Cecile's parents as his own, yet they never dropped their subservient attitude toward him. Cecile had married "above herself" and their awe did not diminish with the years.

Then into their marriage came Anna. An adorable child, she was the pet of the plantation. Sarah bought her a small rake, hoe, and watering can, and the toddler followed her like a shadow.

Blake lived and breathed for his child. He built her a dollhouse with chimneys and fireplaces and mantels and a tiny stairway. From cigar boxes, he fashioned furniture for every room. Cecile made miniature curtains and bedspreads and tablecloths, hemstitching them meticulously.

They had kept her for nine years, nine blissful years with never a thought that the focus of their lives would not be with them forever. The illness—a malarial type fever—hit suddenly and without mercy. Within a week, Anna was a corpse.

Blake clung to the child for several hours, holding her in his arms before allowing her body to be buried. After the funeral, he refused to leave the grave for three days.

Cecile came to comfort him, but his words, when he found speech, were blurred and spasmodic as though his brain was a machine breaking down under intense pressure. "I—I have to get away, Cecile," he had said. "I—I can't explain why. I don't even know myself."

He remembered Cecile putting out her hand and touching his. "Don't leave me, Blake."

"Cecile, you don't understand," he argued. "I must."

He had a desperate desire to run, to flee from this dreadful reality. Cecile could manage; she had her parents.

So he had headed west with a little money in his pocket and the clothes on his back. And now here he was in the New Mexico territory, where the silence ached and tingled all about him. Night after night, he dreamed of Cecile and Anna and the plantation, waking himself with his own moaning.

Then there were some nights he couldn't sleep at all. He visualized sleep as a foe in the soddie mocking him. He would leap from his mat to grapple with it and conquer it. Then, trembling, he would lay down again and call out in confusion, "Why, God? Why?"

CHAPTER SEVEN

The "Sale"

Atlas Teff had done his homework. He had found a devious, self-appointed attorney—one Hal Pratt—to misguide him.

"I haven't worked the hide from my knuckles to let a snippet of a girl have the property that is mine by right," he hissed to the lawyer. "When she is out of the picture, then I'll be ready for my father's signature on the will."

"Someone will be glad to take your kid sister off your hands," Hal said, "for a price. I will lend you the money to rid yourself of her."

"But what if I persuade someone to take Emma, and she finds her way home to claim the inheritance after all?"

"Oh, you must see that nothing of the sort happens, Atlas. Use your head, man! My suggestion would be that you find a stranger passing through—say, at the coach house—and convince that stranger to take the child with them. For a price, of course. Money talks. Pay whatever is necessary. Make whatever deal you must. Invent the most tragic story you can."

Atlas frowned; he did have a heart.

"If you want my services and your inheritance, you will do as I say."

"Yes, sir."

"When she is out of your father's life, he will make the will to you. It is as simple as that."

Thus, when weakness sent Emrick to bed, Atlas was ready. He made Emma's bo-hole-y for breakfast that morning before taking her to "school." Time was running out, and today was the day. . . .

A prick of conscience made Atlas turn his back when Emrick began to tell the child good-bye. "Be careful, and learn your letters well," he said. "And tell teacher hello, and ask a prayer of her for me."

"Yes, Papa. Will you watch my dolly for me?" She pushed her doll into her father's arms. "Millymuff will be a good baby."

Atlas stepped out of the room.

"I'll take care of Millymuff. But Emma, your pinafore is shabby. Why did you choose that one?"

"Atlas told me to wear it, Papa."

"And your shirtwaist. It is dirty. This is no way to go to school!"

"I'm sorry, Papa. Atlas says there is nothing else to wear."

"Atlas!" Emrick's weak voice demanded his son's attention.

"Yes?" Only the head of Atlas reentered the room.

"Emma must not go to school looking like a street urchin. I pride myself in dressing her neatly. You must find her something fitting to wear at once! This garment is faded and frayed—"

"There is nothing clean, sir."

"But surely—"

"I've had no time to kindle a fire under the wash pot. One person cannot be expected to do all the chores inside and out."

"Then we must hire a laundress at once. Today. I shall not have my beautiful daughter the object of ridicule. Perhaps I should keep her home until—"

Atlas thought fast. He could not afford to have his plans shipwrecked now. But it was Emma herself who saved the day.

"Oh, please, Papa! May I go to school?" she pled. "I have a spelling bee today, and teacher is depending on me. I am her best speller. I will explain to her that you are ill, and my clothes beg washing—"

"And that your Papa is hiring a laundress this very day!" finished Emrick. "Make that clear, Emma." He was panting from the effort of so much conversation.

"Yes, Papa."

Atlas scooped up the small bundle of Emma's clothing and personal items that he had garnered, calling to her that it was time to go. He had the shay ready.

"I will see you after school, Papa." Emma pecked his forehead with a kiss and bent to kiss the doll, too. "And I will let you know how I did on the spelling bee. Rest so that you can get well soon. And make Millymuff behave!" She scampered away to join Atlas, books and lunch pail in hand.

But Atlas didn't take the road to the schoolhouse. He turned the vehicle toward Sommerville.

"You aren't taking the right way, Atlas," scolded Emma.

"School is thataway." She pointed.

Now, Atlas figured, was as good a time as any to break the news to the girl. "Emma, I need to have a little talk with you," he began, keeping his voice child friendly. "Papa is very, very ill. I need to take him to a hospital for care so that he can get well. If we don't get him some help soon, he will die." *I'm doing this for her own good,* he told himself, *and it is true that Papa will soon be dead. With the hemorrhaging, he cannot live.* From the corner of his eye, he saw that his words were having their desired effect on Emma.

"We don't want Papa to know, you see. So you must cooperate with me. You are a big girl, and I am depending on your help."

"I can't go to school? Just today?"

"Not today. I'll find a nice lady to keep you while our papa is under the doctor's care. You may even have to go to a new school, for it may take a long while to get Papa back on his feet."

Emma was quiet, but she took the news valiantly. Atlas hoped that she wouldn't cry, and she didn't. "Then I can come back home?" she asked.

"When Papa is well, I will send for you." For a moment, Atlas believed what he said.

"Oh, please, Atlas. Come for me yourself. Whoever keeps me might not know the way to our house."

"As you wish."

Atlas turned the surrey toward the coach house, hoping that he would not have to wait long for someone to take the girl. A tight cord around his chest made his breathing difficult. What if the plan failed?

He was anxious to learn what the "sitting charge" for

Emma would be so that he might make a quick run to Mr. Pratt's office for the funds demanded. He hoped that the expense would not be extravagant.

Emma's appearance would incur sympathy. With purpose he had dressed her shabbily, and even as he approached the station, he was contriving a gut-wrenching story.

"Here's a quarter, Emma," he said to assuage his guilt. "Use it as you wish. But please don't try to write to Papa, for that would make him the more homesick for you and would slow his recovery."

He reined in at the depot. "And you must sit quietly in the buggy while I talk to your caretaker. I will fetch you when I have the arrangements made for your care. Do you understand?"

"Yes, Atlas."

Atlas tied the horse to the hitching post, checked the schedule posted on the door, and went inside. A lone lady waited for the next coach, which wasn't due until noon. Just maybe he was in luck.

Red eyes published that the traveler had been weeping, but Atlas scarcely noticed her swollen face. What he did note were a handsome valise, a chic umbrella, and attire that bespoke wealth. He altered the story he had been creating to fit the circumstances.

"Hello, madam," he said, and she jumped at the sound of his voice. "My name is Atlas Teff. I don't mean to disturb you, but I have a problem. You see, both of my parents have gone on to heaven, and I am left with a wee sister for whom I cannot care. She is a lovely child, well-mannered, and of a beautiful countenance. I am looking for someone to take her."

"How old—?" the lady asked.

"She recently birthdayed into ten."

"Oh, oh—!" the lady dabbed at her eyes. "Just near the age of my own Anna. You see, we lost our Anna— Oh, this might be the answer to my prayer! You wouldn't take her from me, would you? Later, I mean, when you can afford—?"

"Oh, no, I wouldn't do that, madam." A sixth sense told Atlas that his "problem" was solved. He might even . . .

"Would you like to meet Emma?"

"Oh, please. Is she—nearby?"

"I have her with me. In the buggy." He lowered his voice. "It upsets her sorely to mention our parents. I suggest that you avoid the subject altogether." He glanced at her purse. "And another thing. Would it be possible for you to help me out a little? Financially, I mean. With two funerals, it has been hard—"

"You poor man! Certainly. Would fifty dollars be enough?"

"I would be much obliged to you, madam. I will bring my sister to you."

Atlas returned to the conveyance, commanding his feet not to dance. What would Hal Pratt think of this bargain?

"Emma," he spoke gently, "I have found a caretaker for you. You are to travel with her. She is going on a journey that you will enjoy. Don't talk about Papa's illness, and don't act sad. The nice lady is trying to help, and that would make her feel bad. Come with me now to meet her."

Like a sheep led to the slaughter, Emma innocently followed Atlas, smoothing her wrinkled pinafore. He led her to Cecile Dunmore, gave her a hurried kiss, and fled.

He didn't realize until some time later that he hadn't even asked the lady's name. Or her destination.

All he had to worry about now was manufacturing a plausible story for his ailing father.

CHAPTER EIGHT

The Will

The spurious attorney slapped Atlas on the back. "I can't believe you, Atlas Teff!" he howled. "Here I was thinking you would have to pay someone to take the kid, and instead they buy her from you! That is what I call clever dealing. I see that you are a natural-born shark. Fifty dollars—Wow!

"Say, I know where you can double it. We've set a game at Chuckie's Bar for two o'clock. It would be to your advantage to join us. With your luck, you'll likely win the whole pot."

"I don't drink."

"I don't drink, either. Not much, anyhow. I go for the games."

"I don't—"

"Come to think of it, I believe they changed that location. Yes, I'm sure they did. It will be in the back of Mr. Logan's store. Meet you there." Hal Pratt sprinted away.

At two o'clock, Atlas was at Mr. Logan's store, surprised to see how many showed up for the game. Hal introduced Atlas as "a young man on his way to the stars." Time evaporated as Atlas played, sometimes winning and sometimes losing. But when at last the gambling ended, Atlas had indeed doubled his fifty dollars. Now he had a hundred. And so easily! Near dark, he started home with a heady feeling.

But the nearer he got to the ranch, the more wretched he became. Emrick would take Emma's absence very woefully, whatever excuses Atlas gave.

As he walked in the door, Emrick hobbled toward him, spent and shaking. He was still holding the doll. "Oh, I was so worried!" he cried. "I have been watching at the window since four o'clock. What kept you so long? Come, Emma, and give Papa a hug, and tell me about the spelling—" He stopped, bewildered. "Where is Emma?"

"Please sit down, Papa. I'll tell you all that I know. I dropped Emma off near the schoolhouse, but she must have tried to follow me home, knowing that you were sick and ill. According to her teacher, she did not show up for classes.

"When I returned for her this afternoon and learned that she was missing, I knew that she had gotten lost. I have been searching for her ever since."

Emrick's silent tears added to the nagging guilt that now haunted Atlas. He felt wretched.

"Go again, Atlas," begged Emrick. "I would go if these legs would carry me! Search all night if you must. Oh, my baby! She will be so frightened. Oh, merciful God, help her! And help me!"

"I think, Papa, that she is likely to be at someone's

44

house. They will bring her home or take her to school tomorrow." *Maybe the lady at the coach house will change her mind and bring Emma back.*

"Oh, my precious baby!"

"You mustn't fret, Papa. Try to get some rest now."

"Rest? How can I rest?" Emrick wrung his hands. "How can you tell me not to fret when I don't know where my baby, my little Emma, is at this moment? If anything happens to her, I shall not wish to live!"

Atlas heated some broth, but Emrick refused to eat a bite. He refused to go to bed. He prayed and he moaned. "I won't eat a morsel or sleep a wink until she is found," he vowed.

What few scruples Atlas had ate like termites at his soul. If only he had thought to get the woman's name so that he might stop her and bring Emma back! Back to her dying father. No money or property was worth this! With his hundred dollars, he would book passage and catch up with the lady. He would see that Emma was returned to her father.

"I will find her, Papa," Atlas promised. "You can trust me." But all of his assurances fell on deaf ears. Emrick would not be comforted.

Atlas slept little that night. He turned restlessly and rose to sit at the window, gazing out unseeing. Sobs filled the hush of the dark hours, a father's sobs for a lost child. It was as if all the fiends of the netherworld had been loosed in the house.

At morning's light, Atlas went to see the lawyer.

"We must get the papers signed soon," Hal said without preamble. "Your father will grieve himself to death, and we need everything legal in case Gretel finds her way home through the forest. I will come to see your father today."

"I have changed my mind, sir," Atlas said. "I want to find Emma, and—"

Hal Pratt snorted. "Oh, no, no! Don't get cold feet now, Atlas. The old gentleman is going to die anyhow. Dying folks are always emotional. Don't let his weeping bother you. You actually did a noble thing when you sent the child away. Would you want her to be there when her father passes away? Of course not! You did the right thing, the gallant thing, and I'm proud of you. It takes a brave man to do what you did."

Mr. Pratt's words made sense. It would be traumatic for Emma to witness the death of her father. She would be much better off in the hands of a woman.

Yet the thought brought only temporary respite to Atlas. A bur of melancholy still needled him. His father had eaten nothing; he was determined to fast until his Emma was found.

Mr. Pratt came with the paperwork. "Mr. Teff," he said, "we need to set your affairs in order. I am sure that your daughter will be found, but it would be wise for you to stipulate an alternate in your will in the event your chosen heir is displaced. Your son would be the logical choice. I have brought papers for you to sign. I have made certain that the wording is just right."

Emrick, confused and distraught, signed the document without comment or question, and Hal winked across the bent gray head at Atlas. The deed was done.

Atlas would inherit all.

CHAPTER NINE

The Trip

"Where are we going?" Emma asked Cecile Dunmore in a tight, strangled voice.

"I am on my way to New Mexico to see my husband, dear," answered Cecile. "Then we will go back to Alabama to the plantation. You will love the big plantation!"

"But I shouldn't like to go so far away from Papa." Emma kneaded her small hands together. "Papa will miss me." Then suddenly she clapped her hand over her mouth as if she had said something amiss.

The child doesn't want to leave her father's grave, concluded Cecile. *I remember how hard it was for Blake to leave Anna's grave.* She put her arm about Emma's thin shoulders, feeling the tension in the child's body. "We will come back any time you wish," she promised.

"But I can't go back—yet. Not until Atlas sends for me. Not until Papa is well." Again her hand flew to her mouth. "I keep forgetting. Atlas said I must not act sad."

She tried to smile, but the curve of her lips didn't fit with the rest of her face.

"You're a brave girl." Cecile hugged her.

"I wish I had brought Millymuff."

"Who is Millymuff?"

"My dolly."

The bonding of Cecile Dunmore to ten-year-old Emma was instant and complete. She reminded Cecile of her own Anna. How, she queried, could she have been so blessed as to be at the Sommerville station at the opportune time? A barrage of wonderful plans for Emma exploded in her mind. Books, toys, pretty clothes . . .

Emma's unkempt appearance deeply concerned Cecile. *The poor child must have hailed from a poverty-stricken family,* she presumed. *Sharecroppers, no doubt. It will be such fun to dress her in silks and laces and frills.*

"We will buy you a new dress and a petticoat," Cecile mentioned, "at the very first boutique we find."

"Papa shouldn't like you to be out an expense on my account," Emma said. "I have plenty of nice dresses at home. And good shoes, too. Can you make bo-hole-y?"

"I've not heard of a dress like that."

"Oh, it isn't a dress! It's 'lasses and biscuit. You poke a hole in the biscuit and fill it with syrup. Papa makes it for me every morning."

"I can learn to make it," offered Cecile. "My Anna liked scones."

"Who is Myanna?"

"Anna is my little girl who went to heaven."

"How old was she?"

"She was nine."

"Almost as old as me. I'm ten."

"Anna was about your size."

"My mother is in heaven."

"That's what your brother told me. Perhaps she will care for my Anna while I care for her Emma."

"My Papa will care for me when he is well again." She stopped. "But Atlas said I mustn't talk about Mama and Papa."

"Sometimes brothers know best."

"My teacher will miss me. I was in a spelling bee, and she was teaching me my tables."

"We will get you a tutor."

"A horn?"

"A tutor is a private teacher. Anna had a good one."

"Do you have a pianoforte?"

"Yes."

"I should like to learn to play. Papa thought to get me a pump organ, but Atlas said he would chop it up. He said it would make too much noise."

"He was teasing, of course."

"He meant it. Atlas has a bad temper sometimes."

Emma was a strange child, Cecile thought, pretending that her father was yet alive. Blake would love her.

They made a stopover in Dallas. Cecile rented a hotel room, and Emma was delighted with its appointments. She caressed the satin bedspread, the padded vanity stool, and then dropped to her knees. "Even the floor is soft here," she cooed, making Cecile laugh. Oh, if only Blake were here to share these special moments! He would find the joy he had thought withered putting on new leaves.

Cecile and Emma ate custards and pastries and drank

sodas at the soda fountain. With each new adventure, Emma's childish awe flared. "Just wait till I tell Papa and Atlas about this!" she burbled.

"Do you like dresses with ruffles?" Cecile asked.

Emma hunched her shoulders. "I don't know. I never had any. Our sewing lady didn't know how to make them. My dresses back home are pretty, but they are plain. If you would like to buy me a ruffle, Papa will pay you back."

"Anna loved ruffles. She said they made her feel like a princess."

"I could try them," offered Emma. "I'm sure Papa won't care." She looked thoughtful. "And Jesus wouldn't care, would He?"

Cecile smiled. "No, Jesus wouldn't care. He likes for girls to look like ladies."

In the first dress shop, the proprietress fussed over Emma. "What a bonny daughter you have!" she gushed. "She is the prettiest child I have ever seen. That gorgeous hair!"

"Thank you," said Cecile.

"But she isn't my mother," supplied Emma. "She is keeping me until my papa is well again. He has gone to the hospital."

"And what is your name?" asked the shopkeeper.

"Emma Joy Teff."

Joy. Cecile grinned. Blake would like that. *Emma Joy Dunmore.*

"We—my husband and I—are adopting her," Cecile whispered behind her hand.

"I would love to adopt that one!" responded the saleslady, pulling down a soft blue dress with pearl buttons, delicately smocked. "Now, this was made especially for Emma Joy." She slipped the dress over the child's head and turned her toward the beveled mirror.

"Ooh!" squealed Emma. "Papa will love this one! I wish that he could see me—"

"Maybe he *can* see you," Cecile said softly, "all the way from—"

"His eyes aren't that good," laughed Emma, "even with his monocle. Papa might not want to pay such a dear price for a gown, though."

Cecile bought the dress, and they returned to the hotel. "I hope that Papa is getting better," Emma sighed. "And as much as I miss Millymuff now, I'm glad I left her there to keep him company."

Cecile was puzzled. Atlas had asked her not to make mention of the child's parents, that it would upset her. He had suggested avoiding the subject altogether. Yet Emma kept bringing up her father without tears or distress. Was the child in denial? She seemed extremely intelligent, a child not given to fantasy. But denying that her father was dead might be her way of coping. Blake had run, hadn't he? That was his way of handling his grief. To each his own.

One could never tell what was in the mind of a child.

CHAPTER TEN

Leaving

Tired of feeding his father's hopes, Atlas suggested that Emma had likely fallen in the river and drowned. And convinced that Emma was dead, Emrick lived less than a week. "I am going to join Helen and Emma," he told Atlas as he departed, "and I hope that you will meet us in heaven someday."

Atlas shut the door of his mind. He had enough to think about here without fretting about the hereafter. With his father gone, he had no ties to the ranch, and he was anxious to unburden himself from it. He would forget the past and find happiness in a delicious new future, free at last, free to live life as he wished.

And in town, the double-dealing Hal Pratt had plans of his own. The goodly ranch would be his. He had spent sleepless nights mapping his strategy. A fellow as gullible as Atlas Teff wouldn't be hard to outmaneuver. Hal was well stocked with verbal ammunition.

He invited Atlas to another game and persuaded him

to take his first drink, a toast to the happy days ahead. This was a time-honored ritual, Hal proclaimed. Everybody who was anybody celebrated in this fashion. "The drink will relax you," he primed. "It will make a big win more likely. When your mind is relaxed, your natural genius takes over. You have that natural genius, Atlas, but unfortunately, your habit of analytical thinking often overrules your good impulse."

Atlas fell into the devil's trap, proving once again that the love of money is the root of all evil. The game was staged to allow Atlas to win. *He will need those winnings*, chuckled Hal, *to get himself out of town.*

When the young man was well inebriated and elated over the stakes he'd won, Mr. Pratt invited him to his office—a dilapidated storefront—to discuss a deal on the property.

"You mentioned that you would like to sell Paradise Ranch and see the world, Atlas," he broached. "At twenty-six years of age, you are wasting precious time, I would say. Certainly, you don't want to be tied to a tiresome farm a day longer than you must. And I know you would like to be rid of the painful memories, too.

"Unfortunately, money is tight and property isn't turning well just now. I know of five other farms for sale in this area at the moment. People are moving west. But I tell you what I'll do. I'll buy the place myself, today, as a special favor to a friend, and set you free. That is, if you will accept my terms."

He rushed on. "The place is worth eight thousand dollars. You have kept it well. I will give you ten. That includes the cattle, the mill, and the furnishings. You take your buggy and team."

A drunken grin spread over Atlas's face. "That's sporting of you, Hal. That is what I call a real friend."

"The deal is, I can't come up with all the money at once. I must have time. I will pay you ten percent—one thousand dollars—now and make an equal payment twice a year for the next five years." He poked a finger in Atlas's ribs. "By then you will be married to the governor's daughter and living on Capitol Hill."

Atlas laughed. "Or a real princess."

"It's your call." Hal Pratt brought out a sheaf of papers. "To make it legal, I'll need you to sign the deed over to me. Being a man of the law, I don't purchase anything that hasn't a clear title. Bring me your documents and, with your signature, the sale is sealed and settled. You will have a thousand dollars to start your great adventure."

"Thanks, pal Hal. I will run home and get the deed."

"You had best run home and sleep awhile. You have been through a lot, and you may have a little headache. Tomorrow morning is soon enough for business. If I remember correctly, you have a funeral tomorrow afternoon."

Atlas staggered to his feet.

"And since I won't know where to send future payments, Atlas, you can come back to Sommerville twice a year to collect the installments, or send me an address."

"Yes, sir."

On unsteady legs, Atlas blundered his way back to the ranch, glad that his father's remains had been taken to the church. His hands shook, his eyes burned, and a dreadful rush of blood beat in his brain, terrifying him. Was he ill?

A baffling lapse of thought left him stranded, vacant,

and bewildered, groping to pick his way back to a thread of purpose that had been snapped—if he could. The thing to do was hang on, hang on to sanity.

Atlas hung on.

Inside the house, he passed the chair in which his father sat. The empty chair angered him, and he kicked it. Emrick's Bible lay open. *Create in me a clean heart, O God; and renew a right spirit within me.* The words swam before his eyes ere he could turn his head.

Passing Emma's room, he banged the door with his fist, abusing his knuckles. What was wrong with him? He had never been so out of control! He connected none of his violent actions with the drink.

The surge of fury took him, swept him, left him. He fell across his bed, fully clad, and passed into oblivion.

When he awoke the next morning, he had a beastly headache. What had he planned to do today? Oh, yes. The deed. Get it to Hal Pratt, then leave this depressing place for good!

Emrick, an organized man, kept his affairs in strict order. Atlas had no difficulty locating the papers he sought. Snatching the strongbox, he headed for Mr. Pratt's office, and with the headache abating, he accomplished his mission. He signed Paradise Ranch to Hal Pratt and left with a thousand dollars in his pocket.

"I'm clearing out of this town," he told the eager-eyed attorney. They shook hands.

Desperate for flight, Atlas bundled a knapsack of bare necessities. He had money. He could buy what he needed as need demanded. And when this "well" ran dry, there would be five years of more. He would be in his thirties by then, an old man.

He spurned his mother's picture and his father's Bible. He threw Millymuff, Emma's stupid doll, to the floor. He was tacking his sail in another direction, and he wanted no ashes from the past.

He whistled a tune as he exited the yard. He had been liberated.

He didn't even look back.

CHAPTER ELEVEN

Blake's Reaction

As coincidence would have it, Blake Dunmore was in Tucumcari on a rare trip for supplies when the coach bearing Cecile and Emma arrived. His crude wagon was filled with enough grub to last a few more weeks, and he waited for the mail, hoping for a letter from Magnolia Manor.

"I say, Blake," greeted the constable, "I see that you are still here."

"Yes, but I am thinking about going back east, sir."

"It is a bad time to be leaving," advised the officer. "You are sitting on riches out there. You did stake a claim, didn't you?"

"I did. But I'm not sure the claim can hold me. I'm growing homesick for my lovely wife."

"Send for her, Blake. Live out your time on the land. It will be worth it. The government boys are coming in for the oil. There's oil under you. You can make a tall fortune in a short time!"

"I didn't come here for money, sir."

"But money is always a nice fringe benefit. I've never seen anyone with too much of it. If you turn back your acreage, you are throwing away a mint. I would think about it if I were you."

They ambled toward the coach house. "And while you're thinking, let's have some of Lily's good cooking."

"With home-cooked food, I won't be able to think of anything but Alabama!"

Cecile saw Blake when he walked in. Forgetting herself, she gave a yelp of joy and ran to him. A surprised Blake caught her hands. "Cecile! What are you doing here? Am I seeing a vision?"

"I heard that the world's most handsome man was in these parts, and I came to catch a glimpse of him!" It took a great deal of self-mastery to keep Cecile from flinging herself into his arms, but to give way would release the emotion that consumed her. She might create a scene. That thought stopped her.

At once, Blake's glance caught Emma. "And who is this child traveling with you?"

Cecile lowered her voice to a stage whisper. "That is our new daughter."

Blake stiffened; his jaw bunched. "No one will take Anna's place, Cecile. Don't try to push a substitute off on me. It won't work!"

Cecile panicked. "I didn't take this child to replace Anna. I took her because both her parents are dead, and she had no one to care for her save an older brother who couldn't—"

"Send her to the orphanage!"

"Blake!"

"Don't 'Blake' me! If this is your reason for coming—"

"It isn't, Blake. Please believe me. I came to see you! And I won't keep her if it makes you unhappy. But you must give me time to find her a home."

"I don't see why—"

"Shh. We'll discuss it later. In the meantime, please be kind to her. She has been through a lot."

Emma sat on the bench, waiting. When Blake approached, she gave him a disarming smile. "Are you the handsome husband?" she asked.

"Yes," he said, a scowl still fixed in place on his face.

Emma held out a small hand. "Pleased to meet you, sir," she said, her eyes curious. "My name is Emma Joy Teff."

The constable had moved to her side. "And may I have a handshake too, Miss Teff?"

Emma giggled, an adorable little girl's giggle. "Miss Teff! Atlas would think that a hoot."

"And who is Atlas?"

"My brother. He thinks I'm a baby. But really, I'm just plain Emma." She extended her hand.

"And for a nickel, I would take you home with me," teased the lawman.

"For a dime, I wouldn't go!" she returned his badinage, and he guffawed.

"You're all right, kiddo."

"That's what my papa says." She turned back to Blake. "Is it all right if I stay with you for a few days until my papa gets well?"

Cecile shot Blake a silencing look.

"If you will be good. I might even pretend to be your papa, just for now, of course." The gibe of the officer seemed to provide some competition. "You're not old enough to be my papa! Not even play like!"

"Why, I'm thirty-two."

"My papa is sixty-two."

"Well, Anna, in that case—"

"My name isn't Anna. It's Emma. E-M-M-A."

"I'm sorry, Emma. My mistake." Cecile saw that the child had him charmed already.

"Well, Emma—and Cecile—you both have caught me red-handed. I haven't a place suited for ladyfolks. Actually, I live in a cave—"

"As I said, Blake, I will be glad to take the child," the constable pressed. "I'm serious about it. My Barb would love her."

Cecile reckoned that the rivalry was pushing Blake the right direction. "We'll leave that up to Cecile," he said.

"Oh, I've always wanted to explore a cave," Emma chirped. "Please don't let him take me, Mr. Husband!"

"Just buy us a cot, Blake, and we will try your cave," Cecile said. "I will be returning to the plantation soon, anyway. A bit of camping won't turn me to a chaparral bird."

"But first we eat," Blake insisted. "Lily's cooking can't hold a light to yours, Cecile, but," he turned to Emma, "this young lady looks famished."

"I am hungry," responded Emma.

"And what might you like to eat?"

"I wonder, do they make bo-hole-y here?"

"Well, now, I haven't seen that on the menu, but we can ask."

"If I can have a biscuit and 'lasses, I could try to make my own."

ELEVEN / BLAKE'S REACTION

Emma sat beside Blake, smotheringly close. Reared with menfolk all her life, she felt no discomfort in a man's company. She conversed with him so freely that Cecile was often left out.

By the time they climbed into the wagon to go west to Blake's land, the day was far spent. "Look!" cried Emma in childlike delight. "There's a new moon." The silver orb hung suspended in the deepening blue of the sky, attended by an evening star. "And I get to make a wish on that star! I can't tell you what I wish, or it won't come true. But it's about my papa."

Cecile had no need for a star. Her wish had already come true. She offered a prayer of thanks in her heart as she watched a paternal thread begin its weaving between a bereaved father and the orphaned child.

CHAPTER TWELVE

A Matter of the Heart

Atlas left his wagon; it was too cumbersome. All he needed was a fast horse, a horse fast enough to outdistance a scathing conscience and biting memories. He ran in panic as one trapped by the sea on whom the tide advances. Chasing him were the dying cries of his father and Emma's innocent eyes when he "sold" her at the stage stop.

So he ran. He had no destination. But he had money....

For some time, he traveled east, stopping and starting as his moods dictated. But at last he grew tired of roaming, took a room at a place called Carlton Cove, and went to work on a riverboat. There were games and recreation aboard the *Pueblo Queen*, and Atlas lost more money than he made. The tricks that Hal Pratt taught him in Sommerville didn't work.

Thoughts of Emma mixed more and more with his musing, distressing him, robbing his nights of rest. How could he have known that his past would become thorns of self-reproach? He had hoped to enjoy his inheritance, to live splendidly. But he was miserable.

Then one evening, walking past the park, Atlas suddenly didn't want to return to his stifling room. The night was cool, the smell of fresh grass and flowers in the air. Atlas turned into the park.

Couples wandered arm in arm, some sitting closely together on benches, some sharing a picnic basket. Atlas was overtaken by an ache of desolation. Where was his life going?

Then on a bench under a maple tree, he saw her. She had removed her hat and leaned against the seat, her eyes half closed. She was alone.

"May I share this bench?" he said, and she nearly jumped off the seat.

"I'm sorry. I didn't mean to frighten you." He bowed as if to leave. "Perhaps you'd rather not have me."

"Don't go," she said.

"Then it is all right for me to join you?"

"Please," she blurted in a quick, frank manner. "I know who you are."

At once Atlas realized this young lady was the one he had been looking for, a simple, direct, friendly girl. "And how do you know me?"

"You work on my father's boat."

"Your father owns the *Pueblo Queen*?"

"Yes. That is, he is part owner. But it isn't such a nice place to work, is it?"

"It is—a job."

Atlas was certain he had never seen this lady before, or he would certainly remember her. One couldn't forget eyes like purple pansies, hair like spun silk, and skin as flawless as satin, all tied in a just-right package.

"But I'm sorry, I don't know your name," she said.

"I'm Atlas Teff."

"And I am Alice Nugget."

And what a nugget I've found! thrilled Atlas. Atlas and Alice . . . He had fallen in love.

Day after day, they met in the park, and day after day Atlas's fondness for her blossomed. When in her presence, he was lifted out of himself, out of the quicksand of depression, beyond the darkness of spirit and the intolerable oppression of his mind. As a streetlamp breaks the night into periods of light, the measureless blackness of his dejection was gone when he was with her. Not often now, with their immense and crushing weight, did those old and suffocating clouds of misery descend upon him. If only this feeling could last forever!

Thus he gradually evolved into a state in which the past seldom troubled him at all. The apprehensive, tormented look fled from his eyes, and sometimes he smiled.

"I love it when you smile!" Alice encouraged. "Please smile more often."

As a convalescent, after much pain, many fears, and nights void of sleep, is carried outside to enjoy the sunshine, so Atlas rested from his mind's torture. His hands no longer shook, and drink did not tempt him.

Atlas could scarcely pull himself away from Alice, wanting to bask in the refuge from all the demons that devoured him. Here he was, rethinking life, restructuring his future, quietly resolving what should follow.

He was finding peace now, but some attribute was missing. There was yet an emptiness, and he was a thousand leagues removed from true happiness. Happiness was an active thing, a pulsing, living thing, a warm thing. His heart was still barren. But Alice would fill the vacancy. Yes, Alice was the answer.

He would marry her. With the inheritance money coming every six months, he could support her well.

He asked her to dinner and proposed. "I love you, Alice," he said.

"I love you, too, Atlas. More than anything. More than anybody. But I cannot marry you . . . yet."

Alice, a sage woman, saw beneath the layers of pseudo-contentment to the chafing within Atlas. Something was hunting and driving the man. Regret and remorse stalked him.

"Why will you not marry me now?" he cried, weak with desire for her.

"One lives in the world he builds for himself, Atlas," she said slowly, picking her words. "Inside, you are a miserable and unhappy man. Why, I do not know. But marrying me—or anyone else—will not make you happy. It will only heap your misery upon me."

It came out then, the story. "I sent my ten-year-old sister away with a stranger so that I might have my father's ranch," he said bitterly. "My father grieved himself to death for the child, though death would have had its way eventually. Money I have, aplenty. Peace, I haven't."

"Until you right the wrong, Atlas, all the fabric of your life cants on a moldering foundation." Honesty was Alice's tack. "Your house will crash. Our house will crash. I cannot marry you until you settle things with the man who lives within you."

So madly in love was Atlas that he cajoled. "I will make everything right, Alice! It is a promise. I will find my sister and give to her the rightful inheritance. Then I will start anew as a common laborer with you beside me."

"Words are meaningless, Atlas." She drew away from him. "When your slate is cleared, then we will talk marriage."

Atlas wept.

"But just remember one thing, Atlas. I love you with all my heart, and there will never be another man for me. Postponing our union is the hardest thing I have ever done. I am torn. But it is for the best for both of us."

Atlas left Carlton Cove the next day for Sommerville. He had been gone six months, and it was time to collect another installment anyway. This payment, and all future payments, would go to Emma. That was what his father wished.

Days and nights melded together. Rarely did Atlas halt for rest or refreshment. He had but one goal, to rectify the past and get back to Alice.

Alice, his beautiful nugget . . .

CHAPTER THIRTEEN

Breaking
the News

The prairie fascinated Emma.

"Look, Mr. Blake!" she held a baby rabbit whose mother had provided breakfast for a coyote. "I named him Tootles."

She hunted arrowheads until she had an impressive collection. She became gloriously tanned, her golden hair highlighted by the sun, making her the more beautiful. Vibrant health flowed in her blood.

Blake delighted her with stories at night as they watched the moon rise and stars shoot across the sky. Emma enjoyed the fairy tales, but she liked the Bible stories best. "She is a realist," Blake told Cecile. "She can identify fantasy in a heartbeat, yet she understands the difference between fiction and real miracles. She is a special child."

Indeed, Emma was a unique child, mending their hearts in a unique way.

"Prayers aren't always answered the way we expect,

are they, Blake?" Cecile offered one day while Emma played in the sand. "There is our way of reckoning how things ought to be done, and there is God's way. We thought we would never see another happy day when we laid our Anna away. Then God put Emma into our lives. Our Emma came to us as a blessing straight from heaven." She turned toward her husband to see what effect her implication to "our Emma" might have upon him.

"Yes, Cecile," he nodded in agreement. "We have been uncommonly blessed. Emma will never be Anna. She will never take Anna's place. But then, we wouldn't want her to. We want Emma to be her own individual self, and we will love her for who she is, our second daughter. I feel like I am in touch with the world again."

Perhaps because Blake had opened his heart to Emma, he supposed that Emma felt the same way. Therefore, it came as a shock when he found the child sitting alone in the wagon weeping as though her small heart would break.

"Why, Emma! Why are you crying, dear? Have you injured yourself?" He laid a hand on her shoulder.

"N—no!" she sobbed. "I just want to go—to go back home and see Papa. You are good to me, and I like it here, but—but—" Tears coursed down her cheeks.

Cecile had warned him that Emma was in denial about the death of her father. In everything else, she was logical, straightforward. Blake could not understand the phantasm, but the record must be set straight.

"Emma, your papa has gone to heaven."

"He died?"

"Yes, honey."

"Oh, no! Oh, no!" Her whole body convulsed with the

violence of her crying. "I didn't want him to die. I—I wanted him to get well so I could tell him—tell him about Tootles! How do you know he died, Mr. Blake?"

"Your brother told Cecile. Would you like to go back to live with your brother?" *Oh, God, will we have to part with this child, too?* Blake's throat constricted.

Behind her tears, Emma's eyes narrowed. "Oh, sir, I couldn't do that! Atlas doesn't know how to lace my shoes or tie my hair ribbon. He would send me to school looking like a street urchin. And he hates making mixed-up-stirred for me. I think he doesn't like girls at all. But why didn't someone tell me that my papa died?"

"I think your brother asked Cecile not to talk about it."

"Then, I have no home—"

"You can live with Cecile and me."

"Can I live with you for always?"

"Cecile and I would be overjoyed to have you forever, Emma Joy. Which brings us to another question. Would you like to keep your name as Teff, or do you want it changed to Dunmore to match ours?"

"I guess we should all be named the same, shouldn't we?"

"That would be less complicated. And if it is all right with you, we would like to legally adopt you. That way, you would be our heir, and you would be taken care of financially when we are gone."

"Which will be a long time from now because you are only thirty-two. You aren't much older than my brother."

"I'm sorry about your papa, Emma."

"He was a good papa. I know he is happy to be with Mama. And we had a baby that went to heaven, too. He was my twin."

"You had a twin?"

"Yes, but he didn't live long enough to get a name. Now they're all up there with your little girl, aren't they?"

Choked with emotion, Blake changed the subject. "You and your new mama will be going back to the plantation."

"Oh, no, please! Let us stay here with you."

"That would mean we'd have to build a house."

"Oh, let's!"

"And order schoolbooks for you."

"Yes! Yes!"

"When you get older, we will be obliged to send you back east to a finishing school."

"That would be okay. Will Mama Cecile be happy to stay here away from her pretty plantation?"

"Wherever you and I are, she will be content."

"Who will take care of the plantation?"

"Cecile's mother and father are there. If you and Cecile stay, we will all go home together when the homesteading is over."

"It's a deal!" She danced a little jig. Then she stood very still and turned her face. "Will you feel bad if I cry awhile longer? Tears make my sad times easier. It's when I can't cry that I'm the saddest."

"Cry all you need to, Emma. You are a brave girl. I cried for weeks and weeks when I lost my Anna. I would still be crying if it weren't for you. You have filled an empty spot in my heart, and I hope that I may do the same for you."

CHAPTER FOURTEEN

The Picture

Cecile had one sister, Bernadette, eight years her senior. She hardly knew her older sibling, for Bernadette ran away with a Union soldier at age sixteen when Cecile was only eight years old.

She'd borne a son, then left her husband to join a traveling circus, dragging the boy with her. When she tired of the circus, she went on stage. Bernadette was talented and attractive, but she was also worldly minded and materialistic. She hadn't the stuff of a mother in her chromosomes. Over the years, she often left her child with her mother, Sarah, for long periods of time.

Winston Lee Wyford was an incorrigible child. His mother hadn't the time or interest to discipline him, and his grandmother didn't have the heart. Therefore, he was left mostly to chart his own course in life. And that course, decided Cecile, was the way of least resistance.

Winston (the family called him Lee) was born six years before Cecile's Anna, and as Anna grew, so did

Lee's antagonism for her. Anna, a tot who loved everybody, adored her cousin. She could not comprehend that his acts were spiteful. When he pulled her braids or splashed mud on her stockings, she cried pitifully, bringing an irate Cecile to the scene to scold the offender and comfort the offended.

Such scenes were repeated many times a day until Cecile demanded that Bernadette come for her unruly child. If he could not behave, he was not welcome at Magnolia Manor.

Bernadette, as ruffled as an old hen, would take him away, leaving none but Anna to weep for him when he was gone. But when the delinquent mother tired of her fractious son again, this chapter of Cecile's life was repeated. It happened over and again until Anna's death.

The last daguerreotype Cecile had made of her daughter included Lee. Cecile hadn't wanted him in the picture, but Anna insisted to the point of pleading. "Please, Mama!" she begged. "Let Lee come, too."

Admittedly, Lee was a handsome lad, and the portrait turned out deceptively lovely. Anna was dressed in a frothy pink frock of copious ruffles, and Lee was outfitted in a black Dorset suit. It was Anna's favorite photograph.

Cecile kept the picture in her Bible, and one day when she opened the Book to read a scripture to Emma, Emma saw it. "Whose is the likeness?" she asked.

"That is our Anna," answered Cecile. "It is the last picture we have of her."

"She is pretty."

"We thought so."

"But who is the boy? Did you have a boy, too?"

"No, that is my nephew, my sister's son. His name is Lee. He was Anna's cousin."

"Then he is my cousin now?"

"He is," answered Cecile, "your adopted cousin." Her voice was not altogether pleasant.

"I shall get to meet him at the plantation?"

Cecile sighed. "Yes, I'm sure you will. But he is not good company. Lee has a sassy mouth and a disagreeable temper. Many times he made Anna cry with his tormenting."

"Like my brother," supplied Emma. "Then I should be glad that this Lee fellow is not really akin to me. Perhaps that will excuse me from his attention. I will say, 'Lee, I am not your real cousin,' and I will go to my room when he comes to the plantation."

"That might be wise, Emma," Cecile agreed. "But if you ever meet Lee, you must take care that he not deceive you. He can seem very pious, very proper. But it is all a front to get his way."

Emma still gazed at the picture. "Nevertheless, it is a lovely portrait."

CHAPTER FIFTEEN

The Disappointment

Atlas reached the ranch as dusk stole across the fields and massed ahead of him. Walking over the land, he thought he had never seen the place so fair. The harvest-stripped earth lay cool and sweet in the late evening. The girdle of trees that bounded it gleamed with fiery tongues of sumac, flashed with the orange and lemon and brown of the shinnery.

For a moment, he wished he hadn't let the farm go. Even now, he might talk with Hal Pratt and arrange to reimburse the down payment Hal had made. He could bring Alice here, work for Emma, and they would all have a good living. Alice would love Emma. . . .

On the porch sat a tall gentleman, legs stretched before him. He was a stranger to Atlas. Bringing his steed to a halt, Atlas dismounted and approached the stoop.

"Hello. I am Atlas Teff."

"Lonnie Huddleston, here. Help ya?"

"This is my old homeplace."

"Sorry. Didn't know the former occupants. Bought the place six months back from a Mr. Pratt. Paid a ghastly price for it—fifteen grand. Have had nothing but rotten luck since." Mr. Huddleston abbreviated all his sentences. "When bode you here?"

"I was born in the house. My father built it. He passed on a few months ago."

"That figures. Lots of things left in the house. Sent most of them to the poorhouse people. Kept a picture and a Bible and a doll. They yours?"

"I—think so."

"Welcome to take them."

"I will be glad to get them, sir. And I hope to see Mr. Pratt while I am here. He owes me some money."

"Good luck." Mr. Huddleston looked skeptical. "Haven't seen him since he brought the deed and snatched his money."

"I will go into town, get a room, and see him at his office tomorrow."

"Welcome to night here."

"I'm afraid I wouldn't sleep. Papa died here, and the memories are—"

"Yep." The man nodded. "Abide, and I'll get your things, and godspeed."

He shuffled into the house and came back with a burlap bag.

"Thanks." Atlas took the sack.

In Sommerville, he procured a room. Mr. Huddleston's information was gratifying. Since Hal Pratt sold the ranch for cash, he would have the money to pay the entire debt he owed Atlas. After all, he had realized a nice profit.

Plans unrolled in Atlas's mind. When his business was

settled with Mr. Pratt, he would go to the coach house, check the records of the travelers on the date branded in his mind, and learn the destination of the lady who took Emma. It shouldn't be difficult since she was the only passenger that day. Afterward, he would take the proceeds from the ranch—every penny—and give them to Emma. With everything settled, he would go back to Alice.

Upon these tenets, he slept like one drugged. There was but one short sheet of darkness between him and victory.

However, by morning, he found Mr. Pratt's office locked and boarded. Dust shrouded the windowpanes. Upon inquiry, Atlas learned that Mr. Pratt had been gone for some while and that he left no forwarding address. It was rumored that he had taken himself overseas.

Baffled, Atlas spurred his horse toward the ranch. "Mr. Pratt broke his contract with me," he explained to Mr. Huddleston. "Since he did not pay me for the property, it still belongs to me."

"Sorry, son, but that is between you and Pratt," sympathized Mr. Huddleston. "Me, I think the man a shyster, but I paid him square. I hold the papers to the place. Law is on my side."

Numb with shock, Atlas faced the truth: he had been worsted by Hal Pratt. He had lost everything. He had sold his lovely Paradise for a measly thousand dollars! He would never see another penny!

Possessed of tumultuous thoughts, he made his way back to town. He had to find Emma! He had squandered her inheritance, but he would make it up to her somehow. He was young. He was strong. He had the rest of his life to repay her.

He hurried to the coach house—and stopped dead in his tracks. The depot was gone, razed by fire. Only a heap of ashes showed where it had stood. A temporary booth had been set up in the livery stable. He went there.

"I'm trying to locate a passenger," he told the agent. "She came through six months ago on the fifteenth day of—"

"My apologies, sir," the agent shook his head. "All records were lost in the burnout. Our log book, our register, everything." He threw out his hands. "We have no way of knowing who came by, when, or their destination."

"A woman with a parasol and a small girl . . ."

"Sorry, but I can't help you."

Something shattered in Atlas. Now there was no way to make things right. Ever. He had lost his Alice. The string of hope snapped.

He went to the bar and ordered a drink. Then another. And another. When he came to himself, he was propped against a tree, and his mind whirled in gross darkness through which his eyes sought desperately to peer, his hands frantically groping. He tried to reach back to something, to anything he could remember or thought he could remember.

The sheriff came. "Are you drunk, son?"

Atlas stared at him uncomprehending. "I—I don't know what happened to me, sir. I think mayhap I fell from my horse and struck my head. It hurts."

"I think you fell off your rocker," scoffed the officer. "You reek!" He caught Atlas by the arm roughly. "Take yourself away quickly, or I'll take you away. It's your choice."

"A—all right. I'll go! I'll go!"

FIFTEEN / THE DISAPPOINTMENT

Atlas got up and moved away with a sidewinding gait, his brain bewildered. He imagined that someone was following him. He caught his breath, watching from the corner of his eye. The image was his own shadow. He ran, and the shadow man ran with him. He stopped and stood still. The other self stopped also, halting a little behind him. Glancing back, Atlas saw a trash cart overtaking him, brush and debris piled high. He stepped off the paving and started across the road. He judged the distance at which the shadow man trailed him. When the shadow was even with the cart—and he a pace or two beyond—he suddenly turned back and rushed for the pavement again.

"Now I'll be rid of you!" he muttered to the shadow, but it was himself that the shaft struck a glancing blow, throwing him into the path of the horse, who shied to one side. So dizzy was he that he scarcely heard the curses hurled at him by the driver as the cart lurched on, leaving him groaning with the bruises he had suffered. And the shadow was still there.

Atlas tottered along, aimlessly, into the open country. He had lost his horse, he knew not where. Night came, and still he staggered ahead, his progression no more than a labored drag of one foot in front of the other. Finally, he stumbled on a grassy roadside, fell, and slept.

The marching hours brought him to a new day, to a retching sickness and sobriety. It was then he discovered that his money was gone.

He was penniless. All he had now were the three items in the gunny sack: his mother's picture, his father's Bible, and Emma's doll. How he had managed to hold to them, he did not know.

CHAPTER SIXTEEN

Incarceration

By the time Atlas reached a city and civilization, his stomach gnawed with hunger. The day waned, and most of the downtown businesses had closed for the day. He had lost track of time, knowing neither the day of the week nor the month. Nothing mattered now but food.

Behind an old brownstone store, he found a dump pile full of rotting vegetables with which he abated his appetite. Then he found a narrow niche between two buildings, where he curled up to sleep.

About midnight, a boot met his ribs. "Out of here, you bum! We don't allow vagrants in our town," a night watchman barked, thumping his head with a billy club.

Half asleep, Atlas reeled away, and another night brought him into a company of vagabonds more wretched than himself. They shared their bottle and their stolen bread with him. He followed them to the gutters of the city, though he had no idea where he was.

Once a utopia in his mind, city life now became hades

for his soul. His dream became a nightmare.

At length, he ended up in a cell, a miserable jailhouse, accused of assault and battery. He could not recall what he had done or to whom, but he supposed it was a dreadful act. The unknown deed terrified him. How long was his sentence? Forever? He had no advocate and no friend, and as the weeks wore on, he despaired of release.

Without liquor, his mind cleared. What had happened to his burlap bag? Had he lost the only thing on earth that meant anything to him? Old demons of memory came with temperance. Emrick. Emma. Alice. They screamed and indicted and called to account in his head, and just when he thought he might lose his mind, he was blessed (or cursed) with a cell mate to divert his attention.

His "company" was a tattered youth whose skinny body terminated in one good brown boot and a black one through which a toe protruded. His hair reminded Atlas of a porcupine.

"Yee-ha!" the man shouted, irritatingly and often. "What serve they for meals here now, my brother?"

"Gruel."

"Sounds good to me. Yee-ha!"

"It isn't as good as it sounds."

"You can call me Hatter. That's what everybody calls me. They think I'm mad."

"Yee-ha." Atlas supplied drily.

"Now, that's *my* word!" scolded the young man. "You can't have it. It's my magic, you see. Other people have bad times. Burdens. Misfortunes. Me? No cares! No troubles! I always say I won't come here again. But if I didn't, they'd fire me. Well, laugh!"

Atlas moved to the other side of the cell.

SIXTEEN / INCARCERATION

"Afraid of me, huh? What's your name?"

"Atlas."

"The strong man? The man who carried the world on his shoulders?"

"No."

"What's your real name?"

"That is my real name."

"Don't fear me, pal. I won't bother you for long. My pa knows the judge. If that doesn't work, my ma will get me out. She uses blackmail. She has a little history book. It works every time. Yee-ha! What is your crime?"

Atlas said nothing. He didn't know what he had done.

"I warrant your story is the same as mine and everybody else's. You've never done anything wrong in your life, and all your troubles are what other folks did to you. Isn't that right?"

"No."

"You don't care what happens to you?"

"I don't care anything," spat Atlas.

"That's wonderful! Yee-ha! I don't either. That makes two of us. The world is full of adventure for those of us who have no mind and mind nothing. Here, I'll teach you to sing. When you sing, you forget your birthday." The crazed boy jumped to his feet and began a one-man concert.

When he had finished, he fell to his knees and made a steeple with his hands. "Now I will tell you my story. I am a miserable sinner. I have outraged my parents, and I outrage heaven with every breath I take, particularly when my breath is drink laden. I can never encompass goodness, for my flesh is ghastly weak and ghastly vile. But I have worn it for so long that I prefer it so. Yee-ha! This cell is not frightsome, for I will be out by this time tomorrow—" he chopped off his tirade. "But when is the—ah, gruel coming, my brother?"

"We have had all the food we will have today."

"Look, brother, this is no place for nice gentlemen like us, young and handsome. Atlas, if you aren't strong enough to get us out of here, then I am. Yee-ha! Just you watch and see."

With this, he began howling. There were yelps and yips and bellows, then maniacal contortions. He banged his head on the floor.

The jailer, a short, red, reckless man, came on the run. Much to Atlas's relief, he removed the insane man.

With the next day, Atlas was released from prison, abruptly and with no explanation.

"John, the poor mindless boy, left this for you," said the jailer, handing Atlas a five-dollar gold piece. "The poor boy got hold of some wood alcohol and boiled his brains some months ago. Oh, and here is your pack. It would probably be in your best interest to leave our city."

Atlas took his gunny sack and left.

Book Two

CHAPTER SEVENTEEN

The Departure

Every year for seven years, Cecile and Emma made plans to return to Magnolia Manor in the spring. And every year for seven years, they found a plausible reason for the extension of their stay in New Mexico. Now they lacked but a few months to appropriate the land claim, and they could all go east together.

Oil had been discovered on Blake's acreage; a drilling rig was brought in and instant wealth was its fruit. With their own hands, they built an adobe house, cool and comfortable. The catalogue sufficed for shopping, and they had no wants.

Emma loved everything about the place: the climate, the challenges, and the seclusion. However, Blake worried over Emma's lack of a social life. "She is seventeen now, and her world is too small," he told Cecile.

Even the books they had ordered for her education were limited in scope. Emma deserved better. Would he have wanted the isolation of the prairie for his Anna? He wished it even less for the second daughter God had given him. Her emotional welfare was his responsibility, his charge. He and Cecile discussed her future long and often.

"But she doesn't wish to leave us, Blake," argued Cecile, her heart resisting the thought of a single day without Emma.

"You could go back to the plantation with her, Cecile. It would be hard, but I could make it here."

"I cannot be apart from you again, Blake. I thought that I would lose my mind during those lonely days without you before I came. I would be of all women the most miserable if I left you now."

And then, as if she had overheard their discussions, Sarah wrote a letter to Cecile. "Why not send Emma to the plantation ahead of you?" she proposed. "I am so very anxious to meet my granddaughter. She would be great company for me. She could go to college in Montgomery in the fall should she wish to do so. If she is the adaptable young lady that you proclaim, the adjustment will be easy and advantageous. We will see that she has every opportunity to expand her social, spiritual, and emotional life."

At first, Cecile spurned the idea. But Blake said they were being selfish. Emma needed a more well-rounded curriculum, mentally and emotionally. They were thinking of themselves, their wishes, and not in the best interest of their adopted daughter. Finally, Cecile agreed to present the idea to Emma and leave the decision to her.

No, Emma said flatly, she did not want to go to Alabama without them. She would wait. But within a week, she came back to Blake and Cecile with a mellowed attitude. "I will do what you think is best for me," she submitted, and the wind vane swung around for the three of them, bringing plans for Emma's departure.

"We will be home next spring at the latest," Blake said. "And we will be together again then. In the meantime, you will have an open account for whatever you need or wish, Emma."

"I have but one request."

"Yes?"

"If I might, I would like to stop in Sommerville to visit Papa's grave."

"Certainly, Emma," Blake agreed, but a frown pestered Cecile's brow.

Emma saw it and laughed. "You need not worry," she said. "I won't decide to live with my brother. Atlas was a terrible baby-sitter! I don't think he even liked me. Since he hasn't contacted me in all these years, I'm sure his feelings haven't changed."

"Can you remember how to get to your old homeplace?" worried Cecile.

"Anybody in town can direct me to the farm. I'll hire a cart."

"Maybe I'd best go with you, Emma." Cecile's voice dripped with trepidation.

"No, Mama Cecile, your place is here with Papa Blake. I am seventeen and old enough to kill my own snakes. It is time that I grow up. Many young ladies my age are married and mothers themselves. I appreciate your concern, but I will be fine. Truly, I will. You have taught me well, and it is time that I test my wings."

So it was arranged that Emma should travel to Alabama by stage with a three-day stopover in Sommerville to visit her father's grave. "It will give you a break and a rest," Blake said.

Emma's emotions seesawed precariously as the bittersweet parting neared. The impetuousness of youth pulled her toward the new adventures ahead while her spirit clung to the prairie's comfortable rut. Confronted with the unknown, the known seemed the more precious.

And the departure was not without tears, Cecile's being the most unrestrained.

"Don't cry, Mama Cecile," implored Emma. "You will be coming along soon, and the reunion will be the more joyous for the time apart. I will work hard, learn much, and make you proud of me."

"We are already proud of you, Emma!" praised Blake. "Our Anna couldn't have made us one bit prouder." The statement made Emma stand taller.

At the station, there was little time for good-byes. The horses jerked the carriage into movement, and Emma, looking down on the upturned faces of Blake and Cecile, thought that her heart would burst. She watched as their figures grew smaller with every turn of the wheels, then became indistinguishable in the dispersing crowd. How silly was this empty, hopeless feeling! She would see them again in a few short months. . . .

CHAPTER EIGHTEEN

The Letter

Emma had not been gone two weeks when another letter came from Cecile's mother.

"Another letter so soon?" Blake commented. "I fear Sarah is resorting to begging!"

"More plans for our Emma, I venture," Cecile dismissed. But with the reading of the message, her eyes darkened and a little cloud of pain fell over her face.

"What is it, Cecile?"

Cecile read aloud: "Perhaps it would be best to wait to send Emma to Magnolia Manor. Bernadette has taken a mad notion to send Lee to work on the plantation. She wants to go abroad for a year.

"I'm not sure it would be wise to have Emma and Lee here at the same time. Lee might get notions about Emma.

"I will look forward to receiving my new granddaughter at a later date, perhaps when you all come together. I will inform you if Lee takes his leave earlier than expected. God will let us know when the time is right. Love, Mom."

The color had drained from Cecile's face, and her breath came short. "Oh, Blake! Whatever shall we do? Can we stop the coach? Can we call Emma back?"

"I rather doubt it, Cecile. She is well on her way by now."

"I can't believe Bernadette would send Lee to work on the plantation!"

"Work? Ha! I doubt if Lee has ever worked a day in his life. 'Loaf' would be a more fitting word. And the reason she is sending him is because she doesn't know what else to do with him!"

"He will be there when Emma arrives—to flirt with her."

"I think Emma can handle herself, Cecile."

"If she will only remember what I told her a long time ago."

"What did you tell her?"

"She saw the picture of Anna and Lee, and I told her if she ever met him to beware, that he was a snake in the grass. But it's been so long ago."

"Emma never forgets anything."

"I could send a telegram to remind her."

"That might be prudent."

"But—but it will be so unpleasant for Emma with Lee around. I had hoped she would have a good first impression of Magnolia Manor and could enjoy her home. But with Lee and his sour disposition, I am afraid she won't!" They were choked words.

"We can't protect Emma from life, Cecile. If she is to inherit the plantation someday, she will have to deal with disagreeable situations."

"But she is only seventeen, Blake! Oh, how I wish I had gotten the letter two weeks ago or that we could halt the coach!"

"I really don't think we should interfere with her journey, dear. What we must do is pray about the matter. The Lord can take care of everything. Lee may decide that he doesn't wish to work."

Cecile sighed heavily. "You are right, Blake. But I worry. Oh, how I worry about our daughter!"

CHAPTER NINETEEN

Memory's Tricks

With the running of the months, Atlas had become but the shell of a man. At first, he thought of Alice often, but with time and drink, her face dimmed. Gone were the last echoes of her voice; the recall of her smile faded to a blur. Now a flask was his best and only friend.

He dare not look back, for his past drove him and marked him and dropped him. He dare not look forward, for the future was a boiling cauldron of guilt. He trembled as he walked by day, and loathed himself and pitied himself and dreaded himself as he lay awake by night.

Remorse maligned him at every thought of his dying father, his unkindness to Emma, his loss of Alice. He shunned people, avoided eyes that seemed to look not at him but into him to see his wretched soul.

He called himself all the vile names he could think of, going through the alphabet, using every letter. If only he could find someone to tell it to—to say, "I am a dog!" The misery went on, swifter, fiercer, dizzier. He was chained to it hand and foot and heart and mind. And he hated himself.

Now and then, to stave off starvation and buy more drink, Atlas hired out for a few hours of field labor. Then after a day of overexertion, he would sit and count his aches, flexing the sorest of muscles to make them bring more pain. For long periods, he forewent nourishment, and when it rained, he would stand in the weather. These fastings and discomforts were manifest that his body was suffering, a payment in kind for his sins.

He had lived through two lives: life that was not his own, and life that was all his own and to none but himself belonged. Neither had satisfied him. Back at the ranch, in the old life, he was never free. In the new life, he was utterly free. In the old, responsible. Irresponsible in the new. In the old, tied down—"tied down" had been his cry. In the new, released. To what profit?

In the old, he was assured that happiness lay in the new. Now the new, having tried to seek happiness, reckoned happiness more lost, more deeply hidden than ever before. Then it had seemed to lie in freedom; now freedom had been sought and it was not there.

Winter was coming, another dread winter. He had almost frozen last winter; another might be his undoing.

One more drink, just one more drink! Atlas fastened his eyes on a pub's placard in the distance. If only he could make it there and drink his troubles away.

He shambled toward the door, not realizing it was the wrong door. A small group sat in a circle, and someone pulled out a chair for him.

"Welcome, comrade."

It was as if they had been waiting for him. Desperate

for drink, he dropped into a chair, trembling like a leaf. The room swam around and around.

Then he saw that the man beside him held a Bible. Was it his father's Bible? No, he still clutched the dirty tow sack.

From somewhere he seemed to hear his father's voice: *For they have sown the wind, and they shall reap the whirlwind: it hath no stalk: the bud shall yield no meal: if so be it yield, the strangers shall swallow it up.*

There was his father on the bed. . . .

There was Emma. . . .

Darkness, darkness . . .

Someone pushed the Bible toward him. "We read in turn," said a voice. "It is your turn."

They were looking at him, waiting. Running his tongue over his dry lips, he gave voice to the words pointed out by the one seated at his side. "Create in me a clean heart, O God; and renew a right spirit within me."

A clean heart? Atlas stopped. He could go no further. He must get away! Why had they made him read that verse? Was it not because they knew his past? He felt exposed, vulnerable before them. They could see his black heart! Everyone in the room knew what he had done!

Let me go!

Struggling to his feet, Atlas overturned his chair and darted out the door with blind eyes and clenched fists.

Create in me a clean heart. . . .

CHAPTER TWENTY

The Stopover

Winter tarried on some of the mountaintops, but the flat country was bright with cacti blossoms. The sun turned the distant mirages into shimmering lakes.

Emma Dunmore, the daughter Cecile worried about, had settled in for her long trip. It was not altogether a pleasant sensation to be traveling alone, bound for a destination of which she had little knowledge, yet Emma experienced a sense of destiny.

She had been aware since boarding the coach that a young woman going solo across country provided cause for questions. The last doughty little driver—the one who took her into Sommerville—was the most blatant, his gallantry bordering on oversolicitousness.

"Here's your luggage, ma'am," he fawned, lifting his hat so hastily he dropped it on the ground. Red-faced, he snatched it, dusting it on his knee.

Looking about, Emma knew a spate of terror. "This— this isn't my station, sir," she hesitated. "I remember what the place looked like, and—"

"How long has it been since you've been here, ma'am?"

"Seven years."

"The coach house that you remember burned down some years ago, Miss. The city fathers decided to better its location when they rebuilt. Is there no one to meet you? no family?"

"My stop here is only temporary."

"Interesting little town. May I show you around?"

"No, thank you. I will find a hotel or a lodging house to overnight."

"Shun the boardinghouses, Miss. There's a nice hotel six blocks yon. Would you like your luggage delivered there?"

"Yes, please."

Dropping a tip into his hand, she ceremoniously dismissed him, determined to use her own resources to find her way around.

From an old-timer who kept the hotel grounds, she gleaned much information. Yes, he said as a straw wig-wagged between his yellowed teeth, he knew where Paradise Ranch was, but Atlas Teff no longer owned it. It had seen numerous tenants since the old man died and the boy sold it. He thought that a middle-aged couple lived there now. A Mr. Arizoli ran a taxi and would take her wherever she wished to go for a dear price. The fees drivers charged were sinful, he forewarned.

"And heaven knows," he sputtered, "why anyone would want to tour such an uninteresting place!"

"My father was buried here," Emma said.

"And you say your name is Dunmore?"

"Yes, sir."

"I've lived here all my life, and I don't recall any Dunmores. That must have been before my time." He scratched his head, befuddled. "But you can't be more than twenty. Surely my mind isn't going."

Emma offered no explanation, leaving the man to his confusion. Suddenly, she was tired, so tired that the thought of rest became an anguish that caused her eyelids to droop. Her spirit was tired, too. She didn't want to talk or think or explain. She trudged to her room, flung off the spell that memory wove about her, and fell asleep.

The next day, she hired Mr. Arizoli to take her to the ranch. The respite had sharpened her mind. The closer she drew to her childhood home, the more familiar was the scenery. The years melted, and she was a ten-year-old again, sitting beside her father in the wagon and waiting for the sight of the house and her father's voice, "Glad to be home, ain't we, little'un?"

The lawn seemed less spacious than she had remembered it. The house, too, seemed smaller, but otherwise nothing had changed. The morning glories still flaunted their riotous blossoms.

"I—I may be here awhile," she told the driver.

"Take your time, take your time," he drawled. "When you're finished, I will take you to the school and then to the churchyard—and anywhere else you want to go. My time is yours. 'Tain't often that I have such a fetching passenger to tote around."

When Emma knocked at the door of the ranch house, a portly woman answered. "I am Emma Dunmore," she said by way of introduction. "I lived here as a child."

"Well, you ain't much more'n that now," exclaimed the

woman. "Fourteen, maybe? Is that your pa out there?" She squinted toward the buggy.

"No, ma'am. That's a hired driver. I'm seventeen, and I'm on my way to Alabama. I stopped by to appease my sentiment."

"To what?"

"My own mother planted these morning glories." Emma waved her hands toward the vines.

"Well, they're the only thing I like about this place," groused the woman. "I'm Mrs. Austin. We haven't lived here but a few months. And that's a few months too long. You know the history of the place, I guess."

"I've been gone for seven years."

"Some folks say the place is haunted. The man who built it died of a broken heart, or so they say. His wife had already died, leaving him with a girl child in his old age. He had everything willed to her. There was an older son who wanted the ranch. The story has it that he sold his little sister—as Joseph's brethren sold him in the Bible times—to a passing traveler so that he might be the sole heir. Then he told his father that the girl had drowned, or that's the gossip anyhow.

"The old mister grieved himself to death for the girl. Then the son sold the place for half its value and left the country. He hasn't been heard from since, hair nor hoof.

"The man who bought the place resold it at a nice profit. And that's when the bad luck started. Lightning struck a horse. A child was bitten by a snake. A tree fell on a man and broke his leg.

"One renter after another lived here and skittered on. Did you folks have bad luck, too?"

"Mama died here."

TWENTY / THE STOPOVER

"Oh, no! Don't tell me! I hope we leave before misfortune knows we're here. And we probably will. My husband is getting restless. It is too quiet and lonesome out here for him. Why, I caught him talking to the turnips the other day! He's used to town life. We're from Pine Bluff. But do come in!"

Emma had ceased listening, finding only a chilled hole where her heart had once been, as if that throbbing organ had been cruelly removed, leaving its surrounding territory empty. Atlas had "sold" her and told her father that she drowned? Her father thought her dead?

At once, she knew she couldn't go inside the house. She had to get away! She abruptly excused herself, hoping that her emotions would not bleed through. "Pardon me, please, Mrs. Austin. Thanks for the invitation, but time is of the essence."

To the school she went. It looked the same except that it had a new coat of paint. Children frolicked in the schoolyard; classes had been suspended for recess. Miss White stood to one side, her arms folded.

"Emma!" Her former teacher looked puzzled, almost frightened. "You can't be Emma Teff!"

"Miss White!" They embraced.

"But Emma drowned several years ago. She got lost on the way to school and fell into the river. Or so we all heard."

"I have been living in New Mexico." Emma noted that she was as tall as her teacher now. It seemed strange to be meeting her eyes instead of looking up to her face. "I was adopted by a lovely couple, and I am on my way to Alabama. I just came to visit Papa's grave."

"He lies in the churchyard beside your mother," the

teacher nodded. "On cemetery work days, I've tried to keep the weeds at bay. Nobody knows where your brother took himself. He didn't even stay for the burial of your father.

"But I am so very glad to know that you are alive, Emma. You were one of my favorite students. I have kept your slate and your chalk all these years. And I am glad that you have come just now. This is my last year to teach."

"Are—are you ill, Miss White?"

"No, I am quite well, thank you. But with thirty years of teaching, I have saved enough money to make a trip around the world. I want to see all the places I've taught my pupils about in geography class, and I want to go while I am still in fine enough fettle to enjoy myself. The school board has a young lady coming to take my place."

The look of one who is seized of a novel idea crossed her face. "But why not go with me, Emma? We would have a grand time, you and I!"

"I would love it, Miss White. Truly, I would. But I am planning to further my education."

"Ah, when you are my age, Emma, you know that book learning isn't life's core. Anyone with half a wit can learn from a book. Practical knowledge and applied wisdom are what count."

"I trust that I shall have all three," laughed Emma, "book learning, knowledge, and wisdom."

"You were ever the rare one. I pray that all your dreams come true, but I would advise you not to go alone through life as I have done—" she broke off the sentence. "Now I will go with you to the churchyard. I'll tell you all about the homegoing service we held for your father. He was a respected citizen with many friends. If ever a man went to heaven, that one did."

As she stood at her father's grave site, Emma parried with inner indignation. Could she ever forgive a brother who had sold her and sent her precious father to his grave with unspeakable grief?

CHAPTER TWENTY-ONE

The Driver

Cecile had said that Emma would disembark at Hacks Crossing. From there, anyone "handy" would take her to Magnolia Manor. She would be among friends.

She arrived at the depot, which was nothing but a bare room with a bench, mid-afternoon and walked across the street to the store that stood flat on the ground, its door open. A dove-faced woman counted eggs behind the pine counter. The woman glanced up between her count. "Four. Five. Six. May I help you with something, Miss?"

Croker sacks of potatoes sifted their dirt to the floor; overalls and piece goods on the shelves were tumbled and shopworn. From the barrels of pickles and sauerkraut spilled an acrid odor mixed rancidly with the stale air of a place never thoroughly cleaned.

"I am Emma Dunmore, and I need a ride to Magnolia Manor."

"Seven. Eight. Nine—" The counting stopped. "The new

Miss Dunmore! We've heard of you, and everyone is waiting to get a peek at you. But I thought you would have black hair! And to think I should be the first to meet you. Well, well.

"Oh, and I have a telegram here for you." She handed the yellow page to Emma.

Emma read the two-word message: "BE CAREFUL. Stop. Cecile" and puzzled over it. Now, what could that mean? Be careful? Should she be careful of the storekeeper?

"Would you like a cup of tea?" the lady asked.

Be careful. "No, thank you. I need to get to the plantation. Will the wait for a ride be long?"

"Not likely. Winston is in town today, and he'll be going your direction."

A laughing voice behind her spoke, "Yes'm. I'll be going your direction—whichever direction you are going. And I'll be glad to give you a lift if you trust my driving."

Emma turned about and realized with embarrassment that she was staring. A young man, considerably taller than herself, was grinning at her much like a big dog contemplating a mischievous kitten. Her heart beat tumultuously as she met the warmth of his eyes. She felt herself blushing.

"This is Miss Emma Dunmore, Winston," the woman behind the counter introduced. "She needs transportation to Magnolia Manor."

A young woman whom Emma judged to be about her own age had followed the handsome gentleman into the store. "I would trust Winston's driving anytime. Anywhere," she said coyly.

"I'll vouch for his driving, too, Miss Dunmore," the

storekeeper said. "Nine. Ten. Eleven."

"Your transportation will be ready when you are, Miss Dunmore." The man gave an exaggerated bow.

"I'm ready now." Emma started toward the depot, where she had left her traveling case. But the man they called Winston stepped ahead, loading her luggage for her.

The girl, a lass with bold, dark eyes, followed Emma, catching her. "Lucky you!" she whispered. "Every girl in the county would like a chance to ride with Winston, and you get the honor! Rah, rah, rah, Winston! That is the chant of all the single females!"

"Don't include me in your chant, please." Emma turned away. "I'm not interested in winning anybody."

"My name is Judith. Please invite me for a party sometime."

"Your chariot is ready, Miss Dunmore," hailed the young man. He took her hand and hoisted her into the conveyance.

"So you're the new Mistress of Magnolia Manor," he said. "I think you will do well. When I saw you in Agnus's store, I pegged you for a most competent woman." Emma could sense his expression, half appraising, half admiring.

"I hope that I shall be able to adapt to plantation life, sir. I was reared on a farm, so it should be easy enough. And I've not thanked you for your kind offer of transportation."

"Think nothing of it. I was going that direction anyhow." He was a comfortable man to be around; even the silences were comfortable. And the ride was a rather short one. Or perhaps it just seemed so, she told herself, after days of tedious travel.

Emma knew the place was Magnolia Manor when it came into sight. The smothering canopy of magnolia trees were in prolific bloom, and the mansion, above the treetops, raised exquisitely and faultlessly, lovelier than the picture she had carried in the wallet of her mind. The white bulk of it, with a surrounding veranda and a tall balcony, lay stretched upon an undergrowth-free garden whose proportions perfectly matched its own. Welcoming steps led to the front door bordered by snowball bushes.

Her driver helped her from the buggy and deposited her luggage in the foyer of the house. "I have work to do, but I will see you later." He favored her with a charming smile.

Something had been said that was not put into words, something that Emma's mind could not reach. Her heart began to pound, and she was glad when he turned and hurried away.

A housekeeper escorted Emma into a large hall with a fine stairway and which opened on both sides to wide, high-ceiling rooms. To the right, a table set with crystal and silver waited. With a home such as this, how had Cecile ever adjusted to the harshness of the wilderness? Only love could have sired the miracle.

In the room on the left, a tiny fire burned on the hearth, and a woman rose from her needlework. Her iron gray hair was piled in a pompadour. She wore a pince-nez on a black ribbon and a little turned-back collar that gave her a prim air. She looked like an older version of Cecile, and instinctively, Emma knew this was Sarah.

"Why, you must be our Emma!" she exclaimed, coming to give Emma a hug. "And how was your trip?"

"Without mishap, ma'am."

"How did you leave my dear Cecile?"

"In good health and happy."

"I am glad you have come." The housemaid had pushed a wheelchair into the room. "I'm Sarah, and this is Cecil."

"Good afternoon, Emma," Cecil said. "I know you are Emma from Cecile's description of you. I regret that I couldn't come to greet you on your arrival, but I am—as you can see—a prisoner of this chair."

"Cecil fell from the loft of the barn and broke his hip," Sarah explained. "We didn't tell Cecile, for we knew she would worry. The doctor says it will be a while before he can walk again, but we are so glad that God sent our grandson, Lee, to help us. Cecil could never have kept the plantation going without Lee."

Lee. Lee? Where had she heard that name? Oh, yes. . . . The "cousin."

"You've met Lee, of course?"

"No, ma'am, I haven't."

"The housegirl thought that Lee brought you here."

"No, a gentleman from Hacks Crossing who was coming this way gave me a lift."

"Then you will meet Lee at dinner."

CHAPTER TWENTY-TWO

Lee

Emma was shown to Anna's bedroom, a suite that would now be her own. The vast, square room was furnished with complete luxury. Carpeted in a deep pile, blessed with chairs wide and cushioned, its crowning glory was the bed, a picture of inviting comfort, the fringe of whose crocheted spread touched the floor.

Evidently, nothing had been changed since Anna's death. Her porcelain doll sat on the quilt box, a miniature tea service on a child's table. *It is strange,* Emma thought, *but the one thing I miss the most from my childhood is my doll, my Millymuff.* Millymuff wasn't showy like Anna's doll. She was worn from hugs and handling, lumpy from loving. Thinking of her hurt, and Emma chopped off the rumination.

The dormer window provided a grand panorama of the path leading to the front door. Emma would have preferred a back view though she couldn't tell why.

Turning to the bed, she fell across it, feeling like a

swimmer who had struggled for hours against a heavy sea, beached at last upon a lonely shore, too spent to be either glad or sorry. She was in a state of utter exhaustion. Her body ached for rest, her mind shuttled back and forth, weaving with its loom the events of the trip.

Lee was at Magnolia Manor. That's what the telegram was all about. Cecile must have received word and hastened the warning. What had Cecile said about her cousin those many months ago? He was crafty. He could make black appear lily white. *Beware.*

Well, Cecile need not worry. Emma Dunmore would never pay homage at the shrine of Lee Wyford!

Then she fell to reflecting on the pleasant young man who brought her to the manor. Winston. A lovely name. Though she wasn't interested in romance, he might, indeed, prove an ally to her. She would show Cousin Lee that she had other and better friends!

She dozed and was awakened by Sarah's summons for dinner. Much refreshed, she descended the stairs to the dining room. The food looked wonderful—roasted turkey, pears heavy with cream, vegetables swimming in butter, and a sweet confection for dessert. Emma felt that she could do justice to the delicious spread; she was hungry.

The table was set for four, but Lee had not arrived. "Did you call Lee, Sarah?" Cecil asked.

"I did. He said he would be here presently. Poor boy. I fear he is working himself to death!"

"I offered to hire more help, but he insists that he can do it all himself until I am able to get around again."

Emma was looking down when Lee entered. "Lee!" Sarah greeted, enthusiastically. "Emma says that you haven't met—"

Raising her head, Emma caught the sly and knowing grin that slid her direction. *Winston!* Taken aback, she turned her head and gazed out the window beside her, seeing only her own pale image in the pane.

"How do you do, Mistress of Magnolia Manor?" The grin spread on his face.

For all of Emma's brave efforts, she could eat but little. Her mind and heart recoiled. The young man's wiliness had begun! His false smile was so authentic he could have fooled a sage. And his charm would draw women as the candles on the table drew the miller moths.

I will not be duped, Emma resolved even as her will resisted.

Before the meal ended, she had learned two things. First, that Winston Lee Wyford was the pride and joy of his grandparents. They doted on him. They laughed at his stories, frequenting their conversation with "Lee did this" or "Lee did that." Second, that Sarah and Cecil would push the two of them together at every opportunity.

"Lee will show you about the place," Sarah suggested when the interminable meal had ended.

Be careful.

"If I may be excused, please, I will retire for the evening," she said, doing battle with a claw of disappointment that fermented in her like some unquiet yeast.

"There will be plenty of time later," Lee assisted in her acquittal. "She is weary."

Weary? Yes, she was weary—and wary. *When Blake and Cecile arrive, I am sure they will send Lee on his way,* Emma judged. *In the meantime, I will go to school. . . .*

The next morning, she found a rose in a vase sitting

beside her door. "This Cherokee rose reminds me of you, with its petals so purely white and its heart of gold," bore the attached note.

It was signed "Lee."

CHAPTER TWENTY-THREE

The Grave

As the summer passed, Emma was not bothered by Lee's advances as she had supposed. All the caution she'd stored went unused. Indeed, he was so busy that she seldom saw him at all except at meal times. But many evenings, she looked up from her plate to find his eyes upon her as if studying her. And always, always he was polite, the perfect gentleman.

Most of her waking hours were spent in her room or on the front veranda reading. No work seemed to be expected of her. The plantation staff had not found a place for her. She was not a spoke in the wheel of its forward motion; she didn't really belong.

On many mornings, she discovered a single flower at her door, and once there was a potted fern. "The delicate beauty of this fern suggests your shy charm," said the attending note. She had no doubt as to who put it there, and she denied (or ignored) the pleasure it gave her. Lee's notes, she told herself, were as absurd as they were agreeable. Besides, it was one thing to enjoy a man's attention and quite another to like the man himself. She was conquering her truant heart, which was so eager to betray her will.

The hot and humid days unwound and rolled one into another like a spool of yarn. She received frequent letters from Cecile with their subtle warnings. She answered them, assuring her worried guardian that there was nothing to fear. She and Lee were like two travelers, forced by the exigencies of the journey into a juxtaposition from which she would be glad to escape at season's end. Her heart was under lock and key.

But with such an otiose existence, Emma grew bored. To abate her restlessness, she began to take long walks about the place. One day, when she had taken an evening jaunt, she entered a grove that lay beyond the fields. The arbor was shadowy and cool.

Suddenly, she realized that this cove, bordered by boxwood and shaded by trees, was a grave plot. A stone with an angel atop guarded a small mound. *Anna's grave!*

A massive bouquet of freshly cut flowers touched the headstone: purple petunias, nasturtiums, dahlias, daisies, and phlox. The mound had been newly heaped, the entire area weeded and neat. Recent footprints made by the boots of a man kept their imprint in the soft earth. Someone had been here, perhaps only moments before. Who could it have been? Cecil was housebound.

A twig snapped, and Emma looked about. She saw no one, nothing, and decided she had frightened a small animal.

A stone bench sat a short distance from the grave.

TWENTY-THREE / THE GRAVE

Emma seated herself, yielding to the aura of peace that surrounded her, consoling and comforting. She had never feared death. It was life and living that frightened her. Sitting in the dim quiet broken only by the whisper of the wind, she had a sense of the years going past relentlessly. What would they bring her?

"Anna," she spoke softly but aloud, "you should have been the Mistress of Magnolia Manor instead of me, but I will do my best to fill your place for Blake and Cecile Dunmore."

She plucked a flower from the bouquet and laid it on the mound. *I will return here,* she pledged to herself, *when my soul needs quieting.*

But abruptly the summer ended. The time had come to make the trip to Montgomery, to enter the college. And much to Emma's chagrin, Lee brought the surrey to transport her to her classes. With his tall leanness and the lurking merriment in his eyes, he at once seemed the most menacing figure on earth.

He offered his hand to assist her in boarding. "But I— I hired a driver," she objected.

Lee didn't look discomfited, merely penitent. "He sends his apologies and returns your fee. He was not able to make the trip today."

A frown puckered Emma's brow. She positioned her handbag between them, settling into the seat as far from Lee as the limitation of the carriage would permit.

"For heaven's sake, Miss of the manor, don't label me a 'fee-fi-fo-fum' ogre!" laughed Lee. "I won't grind your bones to make my bread! We will have a great trip if you will not stiffen your back."

And they did.

CHAPTER TWENTY-FOUR

School

The academy was an oblong building, three stories high and partly covered with ivy. To the west was the library. A wooden walkway ran between the buildings.

Once inside the dormitory, Emma met her roommate, a diminutive redhead who introduced herself as Jadette. The girl had her belongings scattered in a hodgepodge manner, plaguing the room with pitiful disarray.

"Put your weeds in the closet on the left," were Jadette's first words. "The school very judiciously places new students with those of us who know the ropes. I will be a great help to you. I have an address book full of names, possibilities for sparking. By the way, that smashing young man who brought you here, is he your beau?"

"No!" snapped Emma. Then realizing she had answered sharply, she modified her tone. "No. He is my cousin. Well, really he is no relation to me, but—"

"Good! Then I will try to snare him. I was watching from the window when he helped you from the carriage.

I can spot a real gentleman a mile away. They are rare. What is his name?"

"Lee."

"Will he be coming often?"

"No."

"Well, let's get better acquainted," ordered Jadette in a voice that indicated she would officially preside over Emma's life, time, and plans. "From where do you—and your gorgeous cousin—hie?"

Something arose in Emma, something she didn't understand. Why was she reluctant to let this busybody know where to locate Lee? If she had no interest in him, why should she resent someone else's interest? "I have lived in the New Mexico territory since I was ten years old," sidestepped Emma.

It worked. "Are there really coyotes and rattlesnakes and poisonous lizards there?" Jadette asked.

"Yes."

"Weren't you afraid?"

"No more afraid than I am here with water moccasins and hurricanes and poison ivy," Emma answered. *And Winston Lee Wyford.* "I liked living in the wilderness, really. I had a pet rabbit."

"Did you ever? Then why didn't you stay there?"

"My parents—my adoptive parents—will be moving to Alabama in the spring, and I came ahead of them to start school."

"And this—this cousin?"

"He is visiting his grandparents. He will likely join his mother overseas before long."

"Too bad. But maybe I can change his mind. Then your real parents are dead?"

"Yes."

"Do you have brothers and sisters?"

"I had one brother fifteen years older than myself." Emma was tired of questions.

"My father is dead, too," Jadette prattled. "But my mother is yet alive. She is remarried, and I have a step-sister. She is considerably older than myself, too. She is an old maid; she never married. Can you imagine being a spinster?" Jadette gave a shudder.

"She is a schoolteacher. I am sorry for her. She was betrothed, you see, but something woeful happened. Her espoused, who had the unlikely name of Atlas, had a skeleton hidden in his closet somewhere. He went away to make peace with his past, promising to return to marry her. That has been years ago, and Alice hasn't heard from him from that day to this. She presumes him dead, and she has never stopped grieving. I suppose that she will not marry. She says a promise is a promise in life or death. Did you ever?"

Before a fortnight had passed, Emma wished herself elsewhere, anywhere but in the room with Jadette. The girl was immature and annoying. Plus, life at the university wasn't what she had anticipated. She couldn't put her mind to the less interesting subjects. Restlessness short-circuited her happiness for reasons she couldn't quite put her finger on. Jadette's constant "did you evers," inclement weather, and some of the teachings of the professors with which she did not agree wore her nerves thin. How dare anyone indicate that God didn't create the heavens and the earth!

She was in a great strait. To go back to the plantation would be to put herself back into proximity with Lee. She couldn't do that. To return to New Mexico would be pointless; Blake and Cecile would be abandoning the place in a few short months. Where could she go? What could she do?

Then, to add gall to her wormwood, Emma came from her class one day and discovered that her pillow was missing. "Have you seen my pillow, Jadette?" she asked.

Jadette smiled. "Pillow? Oh, yes. I was reading about pillows today. You know, Frederick the Great never, ever slept on a pillow. So I gave our pillows to the ragman." She wound her curly mop of red hair into a night style while Emma stood aghast.

"Frederick the Great? What has he to do with my pillow?"

"Why, I want us to be great, Emma dear. Both of us. I want to be a great sweetheart, a great wife. And I want you to be a great teacher or nurse or whatever you wish to be. We can learn a lot from famous people."

"But—"

"A pillow has something to do with the head and knowledge."

Emma rolled her petticoat and put it beneath her head. She awoke with a stiff and protesting neck.

That was but the beginning of Emma's Jadette-engineered trials. The girl insisted on reading aloud after dinner, saying Ruskin read aloud from ancient tomes for two hours after his evening meal. He was famous.

The drone of Jadette's voice made concentration and study impossible. Emma was forced to go to the library to accomplish any homework. She shrank from the catcalls and whistles as she walked between the buildings.

Then it rained, and Jadette dashed out for a walk, saying the king of Bavaria went out in the storms to get inspiration for the *Niebelungen Lied*. She urged Emma to join her. Emma refused.

Next, Jadette began "borrowing" items from Emma. Handkerchiefs. Small change. Hair combs. Sashes. Leigh Hunt of England had a borrowing habit and never returned things.

By this time, Emma was fed up. But just before her patience expired, she found a pillow on her bed again. "About the pillow," Jadette explained nonchalantly, "pillows are all right. I read today that Napoleon always used them. Did you ever?"

Not many days hence, Emma returned from the library to find all of Jadette's furnishings gone. She had left a note. She wouldn't be returning. She had met the man of her dreams at the drugstore, eloped with him, and had "quit herself" with the dreary school.

Emma was notified by the office that she would not have another girl in her room until midterm. Her roommate had paid her tuition until then and left no forwarding address for the return of her money. It was not legal to let out a room that was already rented, in the event the former occupant decided to come back.

"Did you ever?" laughed Emma in spite of herself.

Hopefully, life at the school would be bearable now.

CHAPTER TWENTY-FIVE

The Telegram

Emma poured herself into her studies. Study became her panacea. She saw no need to keep correspondence with Cecil and Sarah at the plantation. They had Lee, and he filled their hearts. What need had they of her? He was a grandchild by blood, she but an adopted one.

Sarah sent her a card now and then—as did Lee—and Cecil saw that adequate funds were forthcoming. In fact, he fussed that she lived so frugally. She should be more generous with herself, he wrote. Blake and Cecile would want her to make the best of her school years.

Then a letter came, advising that she would be expected home for the holidays. Lee's work had slacked, and they were planning for a gala occasion. The house was decorated, an annual affair, and they would send Lee to the school for her. They'd pop corn and pull taffy. They would go caroling. They would have a lovely gift exchange.

To go to the plantation for the holidays was a tremendous temptation. Most of the students would be going home, and the school would be a bleak and lonely place with no classes to attend. Already Emma was becoming depressed with the steady, gray drizzle that foreshadowed the winter months ahead. A break would be refreshing. But she did not want Lee coming for her. She was amazed at the strength of her resistance to his closeness.

She wrote back to say that if she decided to make the trip, she would hire a phaeton. But she didn't go.

The next missive, early in February, was an urgent telegram marked "Death Message." Who had died? Cecil or Sarah? Both had seemed in good health when she left. Cecil's broken hip was mending nicely. Or had something happened to Lee?

She tore into the telegram. *Come home at once. Stop. Affairs to be settled. Stop.* It was not signed.

Emma packed her belongings, turned in her books (a sixth sense told her she would not be back), and took a coach to Hacks Crossing. A brother of the storekeeper took her to the plantation.

Cecil and Sarah met her at the door, red-eyed and gaunt. *Then it is Lee,* her mind supplied. *Why would they call me home for a cousin who isn't really my cousin at all?*

"Sit down, Emma," bade Cecil. "We have tragic news. A neighbor found Blake and Cecile frozen to death in a blizzard. They had been to town for supplies and missed their way in the snowstorm." He paused to weep.

"I'm—I'm sorry," murmured Emma, trying to absorb her own shock. "To me it is a bitter loss, but for you and Sarah, it is worse. She was your daughter."

"Yes." Sarah sponged her tears with a lawn handkerchief. "Each of us dies a bit each time we lose someone we love. In fact, we die a little every day. Death is merely the final process in the long quest for death. Did you ever read Lady Lackville's verse? I don't remember the words verbatim, but she says: 'I died of everything. Sorrow. Delight. Love. Winter. Spring. They all slew me in turn— and last of all came death itself.'"

"I've not read it." Emma felt tears dripping from her own lashes. She had suffered death several times now. Papa. Atlas. And now, Blake and Cecile. . . .

"We have but a sketchy account of the details from which we must draw our incomplete conclusions," Cecil said. "They found Cecile in a shelter of sorts beneath an overhang of rocks. Blake had stripped off his coat, covered her, and left her there. He was found a half-mile away."

Emma's heart was pinched and wrung by the story.

"The plantation is in your hands now, Emma," Cecil finished. "You are the legal heir. And we are at your disposal. This is home to us, but if you would like to get someone else—"

Emma held up an unsteady hand. "No. I—I don't know enough about the workings of a plantation—yet. Just—please stay!"

"Cecil isn't young anymore, Emma. He will likely be bothered with arthritis from the bone break. He will need Lee to help him."

"Could—couldn't we find someone else?"

"We could not replace Lee. He knows the ins and outs of the place, he knows the work. He has his heart in it."

"And you will want to return to school," Cecil said.

"No, I will stay here and learn as quickly as possible," she said, lifting her chin resolutely. "It is what Blake and Cecile would want me to do. I will do them the honor of doing my duty for Magnolia Manor, where lies their child—and their hearts."

CHAPTER TWENTY-SIX

The Tramp

A week prior to Emma's return to Magnolia Manor, Lee had come upon a dying man in a barrow ditch. The man, clad in tattered rags and clutching a seedy burlap bag, would have succumbed to the acrid cold in a short while had not Lee happened along at that opportune moment.

He was an emaciated man, light and frail, and of indistinguishable age. Lee had no trouble lifting him into the wagon. Once back at the plantation, he built a fire in one of the tenement cabins, housing once kept for slaves, and made a bed for the ailing transient. He spoon-fed him, forcing warm broth and milk down his throat. But in spite of his administrations, it seemed the poor fellow would slip away.

In and out of consciousness, the sick man pitched. Now and then, he gave Lee a wan smile, but he did not try to talk. He lay for hours with wide, staring eyes, submitting passively to Lee's attempts to make him comfortable.

When at last he roused, Lee sat on the side of the bed and took his hand. "You have been through a rough passage, friend," Lee said, "but I believe you will make it. How do you feel?"

"I'm—weak. I'm sorry I haven't said much. I have been thinking." His voice was furred and thick.

"You have been mending, too, while you were quiet. Did you know that you have been here for more than a month?"

"More than a month," the man echoed in a parrot-like fashion and without emotion.

"Today is the third of March. We need to let your family know where you are."

"I have no family."

"None at all?"

"Look here, as soon as I am strong enough to walk, I'll go away. That's all I want."

Lee was puzzled. "Got a name, I suppose?"

"Atlas."

"Hmm. Mr. Atlas, is that your real name?"

"That's the one my family cursed me with."

"How did you happen to be in the barrow ditch where I found you, Mr. Atlas?"

"You ask too many questions."

"I am only trying to help you, sir."

"Don't call me 'sir'! I'm worthless! I'm a dog!"

"No human being is without merit, sir, and no soul without value. If a dog had a soul, I would give him the same respect."

"I was tramping. Looking for work. I heard that a plantation in the area hired farm help. And—well, I lost my way. Tell me, where am I?"

"This is Magnolia Manor. The place is owned by a lovely young lady. I work here, and when you are sufficiently recovered, I am sure that we can find work for you to do, too."

"Why didn't you let me go?"

"Let you go where, sir?"

"Why didn't you let me die? Why did you save my life? I'm not worth saving."

"How was I to know that your soul was ready for eternity?"

"I deserve whatever punishment I get in the next world."

"I pray that none of us gets what we deserve."

With time and Lee's gentleness, Atlas dropped some of his churlishness. But he wasn't out of the woods yet. He caught a chill, took a fever and then pneumonia, plummeting him back to the brink of death.

Turning over the fields for the spring planting and attending the invalid took all of Lee's time. He showed up at the plantation house only for meals and to fall into bed sleep-shorted and exhausted.

Since Emma had arrived from school, he hadn't the leisure to befriend her.

CHAPTER TWENTY-SEVEN

The Doll

The days passed, taking with them the March breezes that tempered the crescendo of the sun's heat.

Why the lack of attention from Lee now grated upon Emma mystified her. She could not understand her strange, out of hoyle emotions or her own taciturn thoughts. She had wanted Lee out of her life, hadn't she? She planned to dismiss him, didn't she? Then why wasn't she satisfied? Neither her actions nor her reactions made sense.

The oversight of the plantation was a monumental task. There were account books and wages and the management of the house. And keys. Keys to drawers, to closets, to chests. Keys of various sizes and designs—locking and unlocking to become familiar with each one. Was the stress making her edgy?

Cecil consulted with Emma often. Did she want to plant more acres of cotton or less? What about cane? The vegetables hadn't been very profitable last year—there was a surplus—but it might be different this year. Every dollar counted. It didn't seem right, Cecil much older and much more experienced but asking her.

Emma rarely saw Lee. Oh, he didn't deliberately ignore her. He still pulled out her chair at the table, opened doors for her, and offered his hand to assist her if he happened to be there. But he was . . . distracted. Was he seeing the girl at Hacks Crossing?

Unable to sleep because of a troubled ache in her breast (it was very late), Emma went to the pantry for some herbal tea and found Lee slipping out the back door with a cup in his hand. Her heart bucked like a mustang and trampled her breath. She laid it to the unexpectedness of the meeting.

"What are you doing, sir?" she inquired, her voice strained.

"I've a sick man who needs nourishment," he said.

Emma opened her lips impetuously, thought better of the words that burned on them, and at the danger of choking, swallowed them. "Are we not paying the hands adequately? Can they not provide their own nourishment?"

"He isn't a paid hand, Miss. He is a—a poor derelict. And if it unsettles the Mistress of Magnolia Manor to share her substance, please take the expense from my wage. When this man is well—if he gets well—I can certify that he will repay with his service. He is an experienced ranch hand. But if—" Lee's voice suffered a small break "—if I lose him, lay the charges for his care at my feet." Lee made a slight bow and was gone, holding the cup with care.

Why the short speech should irritate Emma infuriated

her the more. Lee had been quiet, calm, and humble in his attitude, yet she was more determined than ever to rid herself of this man when the spring sowing was done, a man who sent sharp splinters of frustration through her being. But why? What had he done amiss? Nothing. He had conducted himself as a gentleman, yes, and even as a Christian always. His fine features were undeniable, his manner flawless. The weakness, then, was in herself. She was afraid of her own heart!

As she stood looking at the place where Lee had stood and remembering his devastating attractiveness and natural charm, the vacancy in her life became a gaping cavern. The parallel of her condition was to one who, rearranging the furniture of her room, stares in constant bafflement at a bare corner and cannot determine with what to fill it. This void, this hollow . . . Was it the absence of her parents? or was there another piece missing?

Little sleep did Emma find that night, and she overslept the next morning. The sun was bright and sharp, the air fresh and bracing, the sky washed blue from an early rain. She sat up, but her shoulders sagged. She had missed breakfast.

Slipping down the stairs, she found Sarah sitting at the table, mending something. "Good morning, Emma!" she said. "I was beginning to think that you had joined Rip Van Winkle for a year's nap."

"You should have called me."

"I figured you needed the rest."

Then Emma saw the items lying on the table. Her mother's picture . . . her father's Bible . . . and her own Millymuff. She grabbed the back of a chair for support.

"Emma!" Sarah flung her sewing aside and jumped up. "You are ill!"

"No, I— What—where—?" Emma pointed at the array on the table.

"Lee asked me to repair this old, ripped sack. I don't know why. It isn't worth the trouble. I think he found it somewhere. Those things were inside."

"I—I do feel sick. I think I had better run back to bed." Emma fled up the staircase as if pursued by ghosts.

CHAPTER TWENTY-EIGHT

The Verse

Sober again, flashbacks rode Atlas hard, and ridden by them, he found his bed first comfortless and then distressing. He must get away!

Daily now, almost hourly, his strength returned. He wanted only a little more to betake himself from this place. And where would he go? back to the bottle?

Through the long night, he thought through it all, reviewing his thirty-four years of blundering, cowardice, and terror. And before daybreak, he reached the certainty that he could endure his life no longer. It was not to be borne. Within the shackles of his own mind, there was no relenting crevice through which he might escape to touch hands with those he had betrayed. He had wronged them, and there was but one remedy. He determined, writhing in those tortures of that night, to settle the score.

By the light of day, his mind was clear and empty as though washed clean by a hurricane. What he was about to do seemed natural: to obliterate himself, to dash from himself the bitter cup of life.

He would walk until he found a lake. He would swim until he was tired. That wouldn't take long. Then he would surrender himself to the black water.

Slowly, Atlas dressed himself and went to the door of the cabin. The sun was hanging, a great ball, just above the horizon. Lee was nowhere to be seen.

Atlas rushed out, feeling the soft earth through the thin soles of his worn boots. His eyes, moving constantly, missed nothing. They took in a flock of crows that rose into the blue of the morning sky, a clump of chicory, and a spider's web, red as copper in the sunrise. They noticed a drop of dew on a fallen leaf, the imprint of a bird's foot in the dust.

Since today would be his last day on earth, he would take with him all that he could absorb to have while he slept, compensation for the pain.

He walked faster and yet faster. Then he was running. But soon he was winded, gasping for breath. Dreadful pains of distressed respiration, bursting heart, and a throbbing head afflicted him as he ran. He labored on in spite of them. His bones seemed only gristle, his muscles gone.

He must turn around, retrace his steps . . . get back to the bed! But looking back, he knew he would never make it to the cabin. His strength was gone, his breath short. Ahead of him was a grove of trees. If he could get there—! There where the vultures would not find his dead body . . .

In the green well of the woods, Atlas found a stone bench and dropped his body upon it. The trees, in their newly opened freshness, exhaled their mossy, resinous scents. What was this? a park? He hated parks! A park reminded him of Alice; he had met her in a park.

But no. There were no picnic tables or ducks swimming on a pond. There were no couples walking hand in hand. This was no park. It was a garden, patched with sunlight and pitted with shadows. So peaceful was the cove that Atlas found a measure of rest from his mind's distresses. His hands ceased their trembling. Here was refuge from all the demons that had harassed him. He had set out to end his life, but a new thought came. What now should he do with a life that death challenged, sickness shattered? It would be an ungracious act to deliberately destroy it.

He had missed something. Could he start afresh? Calmly now he could search his soul, where once the question had been a gnawing tumor, a poisoned wound. Hopelessness no longer burned in his brain.

Surely there was hope somewhere. He unraveled the riddle as far as that.

Somewhere . . . somewhere . . . somewhere . . .

Then Atlas saw the small grave. He dropped to his knees and crawled toward it, reading the inscription: *Our darling Anna Dunmore.*

She had been born the same year as Emma.

She had lived for nine years.

A need to expunge his sin from his soul seized Atlas. "Emma! Emma! I'm sorry, Emma!" He clung to the headstone and wept. Wrung out of his lips was a bitter cry, a groan, an articulate sound of his inward agony.

He wanted to pray, but words would not come.

From the past echoed a verse: *Create in me a clean heart, O God. . . .*

Where had he read it, heard it?
Oh, yes, his father's Bible.

CHAPTER TWENTY-NINE

Repentance

While on his knees before the child's grave, alone with his memories, something broke within Atlas. He cried again: "I'm sorry! I'm sorry, Emma!" He repeated the words over and again. "I have looked back. When I see what a wretched traitor I have been, to live and not destroy myself is almost more than I can bear.

"But I will bear it. I see now. I understand. Self has been the cause of all my wreckage—thoughts of myself and no other. Oh, I see it now, clearly, bitterly, and with self-loathing; I see it!

"Today I thought to end it all. That was self again. So rooted am I in self that only of myself I thought, only of sparing myself these torments by death, of ending them so that I would not have to endure them.

"All my life, I have lived selfishly. Ah, for shame! And today, I almost died in self. But even now, realizing it, still it is hard to tear self out of me. Still I kneel here dreading life, fearing life, whining that it is heavier than I can bear.

147

Oh, how deceptive is self, how cunning, how disguised! Oh, but I must see it! Keep my eyes open so that I will accept my punishment and will not kill myself."

When Atlas's confession became a prayer, he could not have told. "O God, forgive! Give me a clean heart. I, Atlas Teff, wronged my sister. I wronged my poor, dying father. Remember that I am new before Thee, unaccustomed to Thy ways. I am not daring to bargain, Lord. All I ask is this: Hold my father closely to Your bosom, and wherever Emma may be, please guide and guard her. I kneel before Thee, willing to suffer myself if I may know that she is spared.

"What have I to offer? I have nothing to offer! Lord, there is only one thing in me that is different. My eyes are opened to my sins. Keep my eyes open! Help me to rid me of self! Help me to know what is self!

"All my life, all my life from childhood, it has been self. Back on the farm, when I was longing to be free, it was all self, self that was destroying me. Ceaseless work didn't rob my peace of mind or my youth. It was self-pity, thinking of myself. It isn't work or trouble that vexes a man and takes his happiness away. It is never forgetting himself that brings him to ruin. I thought I was sacrificing my life and grudged every minute of toil that took from me my own pursuits.

"Ah, my selfishness has been my curse, the undoing of me! It drove me to the bottle. All that happened to me, I saw in terms of myself and no other. Every irritation of my adolescent years, I at once turned upon myself, seeing with my eyes and not Papa's—or little Emma's.

"To see only with one's own eyes, from one's own vantage point, to estimate life in terms of self, that is to heap upon oneself misery. To see with other's eyes, to judge from their outlook on life, that is the secret to true happiness. That is the thing I have missed in life.

"Help me in the small things, O God. In the everyday things. That is where I battle self. That is where I cannot see clearly and self will fool me. To quarrel. To complain. To be impatient. What is that but self?

"Help me to put myself in the shoes of each one who comes to me. Let me see through their eyes. Oh, rid me of self. . . ."

So lost was Atlas in the cleansing of his heart that he did not hear the commotion just outside the grove.

CHAPTER THIRTY

The Meeting

The ploughing was done, the cotton planted. And each day, tangible results of the labor were visible. On early mornings when Emma walked over the land, she thought of a sculptor who watches his finished work take shape in the stone. This was her land, and its production was beautiful.

She had sought a chance to talk with Lee about the picture and Bible and doll. She wanted to ask where he had found them. But the opportunity to converse with him had not come.

In the core of her being, Emma knew that she could not run the place without Lee. Though she refused to give him credit for the plantation's success, she could not deny the obvious. Nor would she allow herself to marvel at the ease with which he kept his eyes upon all things at all times. The laborers. The crops. But as yet, she had not scrapped her plans to let him go at season's end.

That morning, Emma had arisen at five and breakfasted by seven. She was walking over the place, and nearing the private cemetery in the grove, she heard a sound that slowed her steps and then brought them to a standstill. Through the foliage, she saw a man kneeling, clutching Anna's headstone. She tossed in her mind who the man might be and why he would grieve over the child's tomb. Then she heard his piteous confession. Every word of it. *But it—it couldn't be—?*

Dizziness swept over Emma. The world blurred and retreated, filling with blackness, then nothingness. Neither sight nor sound could reach her.

When she awoke, she was moaning. Little by little, her sluggish body was awakening, her benumbed thoughts beginning to stir. Her body didn't seem to belong to her. She opened her eyes only to close them again. How long had she been in this cave of darkness? And there had been dreams . . . dreams of Lee. . . .

Then she discovered that she was lying in the parlor of the plantation house with Sarah beside her. For a moment, she searched for reality, conscious of sounds coming as from a great distance. She pushed her way through the swirls of darkness and sat up.

"Not too fast, dear," Sarah warned. "Rest awhile. You're as white as a sheet."

"How—how did I get here? What happened?"

"Lee brought you in his own arms. He said that you fainted in the field. You are working too hard, Emma, and not eating enough."

"No, it isn't that—"

Had she imagined that she had seen her brother? that she had heard him pray? Was it a hallucination? What brought it on? Was it the sight of her own doll, perhaps?

"Where is—Lee?"

"He is attending a sick man just now. One of the plantation hands, I think. Lee has such a big heart—"

As if on cue, Lee came in. "How is Emma, Grandma? I got the man back to his cabin. Now I'll get Emma to the doctor—" he stopped. "Emma! I'm glad to see that you have revived."

"Tell me, sir. Was there a man at—at the grave?"

"There was, Miss Emma, but he is okay now."

"Who—?"

"An ailing, down on his luck hobo, Miss Emma, that I rescued from freezing to death in the winter. He would have died had I not found him. I have been taking care of his needs from my own wages. None of his expenses have been imposed upon your goodness."

"What is his name?"

"Mr. Atlas."

"I—I would like to meet him. To—talk to him."

"He isn't much for meeting strangers, I'm afraid. But I'll tell him you wish to see him."

"Oh, I must see him! Today, please. Now."

"His emotions are very fragile at present, Miss Emma."

"I—understand. I will bear that in mind."

"At your command, milady! I'll do anything to keep you from another faint. I was terrified!" His comical salute made Emma smile. If anyone's emotions were fragile, she decided, they were her own.

As time hung motionless, a jumble of possibilities romped in Emma's head. The burlap bag . . . the picture . . . the Bible . . . the doll . . . They were from her childhood home. This man who called himself Atlas, who was he? She waited. And waited some more. Was it an hour? Two hours?

At last they came, with Lee half dragging, half carrying Atlas into the room. "He didn't want to come, Miss. But I told him that he must. When the Mistress of Magnolia Manor speaks, her word is law." He gave Emma one of his heart-stopping, boyish grins.

The sight of her brother made Emma gasp. This was Atlas, truly, but he was nothing but skin and bones! He looked as old as her father had looked the last time she saw him. It was obvious that Lee had tried to make Atlas presentable for the meeting. His hair was tamed with axle grease, his face clean shaven. But his clothes were pitifully tattered though Lee had obviously tried to launder them.

"You wish to see me, ma'am?" Atlas's voice was weak, strained, and a spike of fear badgered his eyes.

Emma realized that he did not recognize her. Why should he? It had been more than eight years; she was but a child when they parted.

"I'm not really fit to be in your grand house." He looked at his ragged clothes. "I thought I was able to go today, but I wasn't. Maybe tomorrow. I'm sorry—"

Tears smarted behind Emma's lids. She tried to contain the joy and pain that mingled. "I'm Emma Dunmore, sir. And your name is—?"

"Emma? I had a sister named Emma. Emma Teff. We lived in Arkansas. My name is Atlas. Atlas Teff. How may I serve you, Miss Dunmore?"

The present was gone, the past back again. Emma was a child, eating her bo-hole-y. Then she was at the depot, frightened, being handed over to Cecile Dunmore. Could she forgive her brother now? *Would she?* "Tell me about yourself, Mr. Teff. What about your family?"

"It is too painful, ma'am, please. I have no family. I sold my sister and sent my father to a grieving grave." Tears crawled through the fingers that covered his face. "I became a wretched wino, and were it not for Mr. Lee here, I would be in a lost eternity. But I will go, ma'am, as soon as I am able. Or I will stay and work for you for the rest of my days. You call it."

"This sister that you sold, is she alive?" Emma asked.

"I don't know, ma'am. Oh, how I wish that I knew! I've spent many years searching for her to ask her pardon, but I have no way of knowing where she might be. She would be nearing nineteen years old by now. I have her doll, her Millymuff. It was her favorite."

A sound escaped Emma's lips, a sound that hung midway between a laugh and a cry. She swayed, and Sarah ran to her side. "Emma!"

"I'm all right." She reached and took the hand of Atlas. "Atlas, I am Emma! I am your sister!"

Atlas simply stood there. He did nothing, said nothing. Then he fell to his knees, crawled to her feet, and caressed them. He could not speak, even her name. Only his lips formed words.

At last he stammered, "Emma. My little Emma! I am sorry! Forgive me. Oh, forgive me! Today—today I made plans to end my life. Thank God, I didn't. But I will gladly give it for you."

"No, Atlas. Jesus gave His life for me, and that is enough. From you, I will only ask one favor." She was smiling. Her audience missed the trace of mischief.

"Anything, my precious sister!"

"Teach my cook to make bo-hole-y like Papa used to make for us! And bring me my Millymuff!"

She looked up to find Lee's eyes upon her, tender eyes. The happiness which she had given up for lost swept through her, dizzy and sweet.

CHAPTER THIRTY-ONE

The Reconsideration

Word traveled fast. When the cook learned that Emma's brother would dine with them at dinner, she planned an extravagant menu with stuffed crayfish, pork roasted with yams, hot breads, jams and jellies. She also heard that this brother would teach her to make something called "bo-hole-y" for breakfast. The entire staff was coming to sample it.

The housekeeper was instructed to ready a room for Atlas despite his objections. With Atlas in the house, Emma knew she would the oftener be in Lee's presence, for he still insisted on "attending" Atlas. But the thought no longer troubled her. She would deal with matters of the heart later.

Before the week expired, sister and brother had learned much of each other's interim years. Emma was apprised of Atlas's losses, how he had been swindled out of Paradise Ranch by a glib-tongued lawyer. She heard about Alice and ached with the story of her brother's lost love. *Atlas is homesick for the old homeplace,* she told herself.

"Atlas!" she reminded. "Did you not know that Papa reserved forty acres for you? It has a small shack on it—and water."

"No," Atlas responded. "I didn't know. Actually, I didn't even read the will. It was read to me by Mr. Pratt. He didn't mention the forty acres. But if, indeed, Papa left it to me, I shall honor him by making the land the most productive forty acres in Arkansas." His eyes lighted. "And maybe—just maybe someday I can buy the ranch back. Emma, would that be hoping for too much?"

"No, it wouldn't," Emma scotched. "Let's you and me make a trip to the ranch together. We will see how the land lays, so to speak. We will go as soon as you feel strong enough to travel. If Lee will agree to manage Magnolia Manor until I can get back—"

Lee heard. "I will," he said, "if you'll leave Millymuff to help me. That way, I'll know for sure you'll be back."

"I wish we could go today!" Atlas said.

"With that bo-hole-y, it won't be long until you're strong again," Emma assured.

And she was right. The forgiven Atlas bounced back with amazing alacrity, and Emma made arrangements for their trip.

Lee drove them to Hacks Crossing, taking the responsibility of situating Emma in the wagon. "Atlas isn't strong enough to bear your weight yet," he excused, but a little thrill could not be denied Emma.

At the coach house, the girl named Judith ran from the store across the street, her newly bobbed hair springing with each step. "Winston!" she gushed, laying a brazen hand on his arm. "It has been ever so long since I have seen you! Where have you been keeping your handsome self?" She laughed, a brash, grating laugh, and Emma suppressed an urge to remove her crimson-nailed fingertips from Lee's arm. What right had the girl—? But what right had she, Emma Dunmore, to resent the attentions given to Lee? He didn't belong to her.

Judith turned to Emma. "Are you going somewhere, dear?"

"I'm returning to my childhood home."

"How wonderful! I am so glad for you! I hope that you enjoyed your visit here. Come again some day."

"She is the Mistress of Magnolia Manor now," supplied Atlas. His eyes twinkled. "She isn't a visitor."

"Oh." Judith focused her eyes on Lee again (if they had ever left him), "Winston, I am having a party Saturday night, and I hope that you will honor me with your presence." She widened her painted eyes.

"I must beg to be excused, Judith. I have given my word to see to the plantation in Miss Dunmore's absence. I'm also caring for Miss Millymuff, and I fear I will be exceedingly busy." He moved to the counter to help Emma with the tickets, and when the boarding call came, he brought her hand to his lips, kissing it lightly. "Take care, Mistress of Magnolia Manor," he said. "May your journey be prosperous and your return be soon."

When the door of the coach closed, Emma leaned against it, suddenly weak, her heart smothering her. The palms of her hands were wet, and she wiped them slowly down the sides of her skirt. All sorts of thoughts churned in her mind, and one last call on her heart made her look back to see Lee mounting the buggy, leaving Judith standing at a distance like a hungry vulture. *That one got away from your red talons, Judith,* she gloated.

"Lee is a fine gentleman, Emma," Atlas was saying. "I owe my life to him. He just wouldn't give up on me."

"I have been told that his goodness is all a front, Atlas, and that he isn't real."

Atlas looked bewildered. "Why, he is the most real man I've ever met, Emma. And I should know. In the hours and days he attended me, if he was fake, it would have shown. When he thought I was sleeping, I heard him praying. I've never heard such a beautiful prayer nor one so genuine."

"I'm not sure—"

"And, Emma, he is madly in love with you. Can't you see it?"

"I—I guess I haven't given myself a chance."

"The day you fainted in the field, he found you. He cried and he prayed. And, oh, what a prayer! He asked God not to let 'his darling' die."

"He did?"

"He told me a lot about himself. He said he was quite a rogue before God saved him. But he is a fine Christian now. And he tells me that he will be leaving when the crops are in, that you are dismissing him. He says it will be the hardest thing he has ever done, to leave you.

"I have no rights to interfere in your business, Emma, but you will not find anyone else who works as hard or is as loyal as Lee. His heart is in the plantation."

"I will—I will reconsider, Atlas, if you think that I should."

"Pardon me for saying so, Emma, but you should reconsider several things when it comes to Lee."

THIRTY-ONE / THE RECONSIDERATION

Emma closed her eyes. And reconsidered.

Suddenly, without preparation, without warning, Emma knew that she had fallen in love. Fallen in love with Winston Lee Wyford.

CHAPTER THIRTY-TWO

Back to Paradise

As they approached Paradise Ranch, Emma watched Atlas, reading his change of moods. He was, she sensed, painfully divided between excitement and dread. She understood. It was hard for him to forgive himself for losing the lovely ranch. Hard for him to go back where their papa had died. Hard for him to make peace with the past. Yet he was proud of his forty acres, anxious to start anew. She had no doubts that he would be successful.

In Sommerville, they had heard that a woman, the new schoolmarm, was renting the house. It was occupied as a dwelling only now, the land uncropped, lying fallow. Atlas voiced his hope that he might lease some of the land that adjoined his own small acreage.

The place looked much the same. "It's as if we're coming home from town," mentioned Emma. "I almost expect Papa to meet us."

A lady bent over the flowers, pulling weeds from the

bed of morning glories. As Emma and Atlas neared, she straightened. "Hello?"

"We have come on a bit of business, as well as sentiment, ma'am," Emma extended her hand. "My brother owns forty acres of this property on the back corner. It was left him by our papa. But you will not have to be troubled that he will bother you. He is part hermit—and shy of womenfolk—and likely as not, you will never catch a glimpse of him!"

"I'll be there if you need me, though, ma'am," spoke up Atlas. "My name is Atlas Teff, and this is my sister, Emma Dunmore."

The teacher ran a trembling hand across her face, leaving a trail of black dirt. "Atlas?" Her legs folded beneath her, and she sat abruptly on the grass. She gave Atlas an odd look, then spoke his name again, more weakly this time: "*Atlas?*" She seemed to be searching his eyes for something, some recognition, some solidity and certainty to her conviction.

"I'm—Alice. Alice Nugget."

"Alice? Alice!" Atlas was beside her on his knees. "Not my Alice? It—can't be—"

"Yes." Alice smiled into his eyes.

Atlas took her hand, and her fingers tightened over his. Now his voice hurried as if to speed the reality of his dream. "Oh, tell me that it is true, my dear!"

"It is true." For a moment, emotion choked her, and she blinked back tears, tears that would not be staunched. Atlas took his handkerchief and very gently wiped them, smearing the dirt all over her face. "I've waited for you all these years, Atlas. That's why I'm here, living in your old homeplace. I hoped that you would return someday though I feared you dead.

"But you almost missed me. I—I can't keep up the rent any longer. I am turning the place back at the end of the month."

"You won't turn it back!" Emma blurted. "I will pay the rent! In fact, we—we want to buy the place if it is for sale."

She wasn't sure that the two heard her. They had eyes only for each other and had quite forgotten that she was there.

At once, Alice was in Atlas's arms, her cheek against his. There was moisture—and dirt—on both faces.

"What, are you crying, too?" asked Alice, laughing through her tears. "Aren't we a pair, though?"

CHAPTER THIRTY-THREE

Mistress of Magnolia Manor

Emma thought she had never seen such a fine day, had never been aware of such deep, piercing joy.

The owner of Paradise Ranch had been located and proceedings begun that the property would belong to the son of its original owner. The seller was glad to have it off his hands. Such stories of the place circulated that naught but the spinster schoolteacher would consider renting it.

Atlas and Alice were married in the churchyard beside Emrick Teff's new headstone, a monument the stonecutters had set at Emma's request. It was an unusual ceremony, to be sure, fodder for many hours of town talk. The prodigal had come home, it was narrated, forgiven by the sister he had sold, who was now the very wealthy Mistress of a spreading southern plantation in Alabama. The girl was rich enough to buy the entire town of Sommerville and have money left.

Eyes of the townspeople followed her to the telegraph

167

office after the wedding, yet none but she and the close-mouthed telegraph operator knew what the hasty message said:

"My dear Lee. Stop. Atlas has wed. Stop. Details later. Stop. Am bringing my heart home to the plantation. Stop. To the man I love. Stop. To you. Stop."

She signed it: *The Mistress of Magnolia Manor.*

About the Author

LAJOYCE MARTIN has written numerous books. She has written wholesome Christian literature for over thirty-five years, yet her love for good words has not diminished. She has produced an average of two books per year since 1986, totaling more than thirty works. She is a busy pastor's wife, speaker, and spoiler of grandchildren. However, she always makes time to write one more chapter . . . and to find one more friend.

OTHER BOOKS *by LaJoyce Martin*

The Harris Family Saga:
To Love a Bent-Winged Angel
Love's Mended Wings
Love's Golden Wings
When Love Filled the Gap
To Love a Runaway
A Single Worry
Two Scars Against One
The Fiddler's Song
The Artist's Quest
To Say Goodbye

Pioneer Romance:
Another Vow
Beyond the Shadow
Brother Harry and the Hobo
Destiny's Winding Road
Heart-Shaped Pieces
Light in the Evening Time
Love's Velvet Chains
Mister B's Land
The Postmark
The Wooden Heart
To Strike a Match
The Watchdog
A Promise to Papa
Winter's Rainbow

Historical Romance:
So Swift the Storm
So Long the Night

Historical Novel:
Thread's End

Western:
The Other Side of Jordan
To Even the Score

Path of Promise:
The Broken Bow
Ordered Steps

Children's Short Stories:
Batteries for My Flashlight
Cookies that Don't Crumble
Oh, If Only the Animals in the Bible Could Talk!
Granny Mullins Series on CD

Nonfiction:
Alpha-Toons
And They All Lived Happily Ever After
Coriander Seed and Honey
Heroes, Sheroes, and a Few Zeroes
I'm Coming Apart, Lord!
Little Words Make a Big Difference
Mother Eve's Garden Club

Order from:
Pentecostal Publishing House
8855 Dunn Road
Hazelwood, MO 63042-2299